THE FAMILY SECRET

Distorted Images and The long Road to Truth

Connie Lemonde

Copyright © 2006 by Connie Lemonde

ISBN 0-7414-3278-1

Published by:

PUBLISHING.COM

1094 New DeHaven Street, Suite 100
West Conshohocken, PA 19428-2713
Info@buybooksontheweb.com
www.buybooksontheweb.com
Toll-free (877) BUY BOOK
Local Phone (610) 941-9999
Fax (610) 941-9959

Printed in the United States of America

Printed on Recycled Paper

Published July 2006

To

The search for

TRUTH

CONTENTS

Strong winds travel through eras bringing change, small and big, quiet and thunderous, moderate and extreme, yet it's in stillness that the soul finds its truth.

CHAPTER 1

"It's a surprise. You'll like it. Come on."

August, 1947 "happened" and little Michelle's life would never be the same again.

On that day she was humming as she grabbed a handful of grain from her blue bucket and scattered them around the chickens that were scampering all over their fenced yard. One of the hens stopped, looked straight up at the girl, and then returned to her dining. Michelle smiled back at the daring feathery creature and stooped to give her some extra food.

The girl's father, Elphège Bellerose, had been gathering eggs in the coop when he noticed his daughter through the back exit that was still open. He quit his chore and walked to the door. For a while he stood observing his child, the only female out of five children. She was a beautiful six-year old: fair- skinned, a little tall for her age, with big, curious brown eyes framed by amazing eyelashes. The yellow pinafore dress that she was wearing over a short-sleeved white blouse was a strong complement to her long, dark brown hair that was tied in back and swished around a bit with every motion that she made.

After a few minutes, he called loudly, "Michelle, come in here!"

She jerked around and stopped short at the sight of her father, dressed only in overalls and mud boots, standing stiffly in the entrance.

The day was hot and sticky, and he drew a large handkerchief from a pocket and wiped his forehead. "Why do you look so scared?" he asked. "Did you do something wrong again?"

Michelle's blue pail swung back and forth. "No."

"Well, then, don't worry. I won't hit you. I just want to show you something."

"What is it?"

He beckoned with his finger. "It's a surprise. You'll really like it. Come on."

"A nice surprise?" the girl exclaimed excitedly, as she dropped her pail and started skipping ahead. Her father had never, ever given her anything special and she couldn't wait to see what it was.

In the doorway, Elphège turned around and faced the front entrance as he waited.

Just as the child ran over the threshold, a loud, angry cry came from the front door that had just opened.

"What in the world are you doing?" roared throughout the whole room and the walls almost shook.

Michelle braked short as her grandmother ran in waving her arms helter-skelter in the air. The woman was so incensed that her face seemed to be on fire.

Elphège exploded with curses, stared defiantly at his furious mother-in-law and walked out, head high.

Totally confused at Grandmaman Cecile's out-of-character outbreak, the girl started to cry. Cecile hugged her for a long time; then, without a word, she took Michelle's hand and led her into the house.

When they got into the kitchen, the girl was shaking. "I'm sorry I scared you so much," the grandmother said softly, as she bent and kissed the child's forehead.

"But why are you so mad? Papa wasn't going to hit me! He was only going to give me a nice surprise. That's what he said!"

Michelle's mother, Marie, had been kneading dough when the two appeared in the kitchen. Instantly her hands stalled. "Maman! What's going on? Your face is as red as a tomato!"

"Just a minute, Marie," Cecile answered, and she bent toward Michelle. "I'm sorry that I scared you so much. I just overreacted. You know how your mother always tells your brothers that they overreact. Well, that's what I was doing. I'm truly sorry. Why don't you go up and play with your toys, now. I have to speak to your mother."

"Okay." Michelle wiped her nose instinctively with her hand and shuffled slowly out of the room.

When the girl disappeared, Cecile signaled Marie to sit down. "Come here. We have to talk."

"But I'm making bread."

"It'll wait," Cecile commanded.

Marie sat.

"What does he mean, Maman?"

The next day, Michelle, Marie and Cecile were sitting in a stuffy visitors' room at the parish rectory.

The pastor puffed on his Camel cigarette and listened intently as Cecile recounted the event in the chicken coop. Finally he pushed and swished his tobacco butt in the glass ashtray on his desk and agreed. "Yes, I do think you should send her to boarding school in Canada." He looked at the girl and continued, "The farther away from Mapleview, Vermont, the better."

"What does he mean, Maman?" The girl's words were punctuated with uneasiness.

Marie Bellerose leaned toward her daughter. "We want you to go to school with the Sisters in Canada. You'll live there with other girls and make lots of new friends. I'm sure you'll like it very much."

"But why?" Michelle's eyes blurred with tears. "And who will feed the chickens and help you with all your work?"

"Your brothers will help me."

"But I'm the only girl," Michelle argued. "*I know* how to help you in the house. They don't!"

Grandmaman laughed. "Boys or not, they *will* learn! *I'll* make sure of that. Except for Jean and David of course. They're too young."

Michelle couldn't argue with that, so she turned to her mother. "But, Maman. Canada! That's far, far away!"

Marie cupped Michelle's two small hands into her own. "It's not really that far, dear. I'll write and send you news about everyone."

Michelle's little hands were getting cold and wet.

"Remember what we talked about last night?" Marie asked. "Didn't we agree that we should always try to find good things in life, even when everything seems to go wrong?"

Michelle's lustrous brown eyes looked pleadingly at her mother and her feet shifted from one spot to the other. Then she forced a smile. "I'll try, Maman. I'll really try."

CHAPTER 2

"...but he's old. He (God) looks like a nice grandfather."

In January of the following year, Michelle celebrated her seventh birthday. She had adjusted very well to living in the boarding school. Her ability to laugh and think more of the good than the bad helped her to make friends easily and to adapt to an environment that was, at first, so very foreign to her.

She liked most of the Sisters, although she did have a problem with Sr. St. Veronique who always had her "clapper" stuffed in her pocket, ready to bring down on the knuckles of those who disobeyed or didn't quite meet her requirements. Her very favorite nun, however, was Sr. St. Clara who was never too busy to listen to her and always made Michelle feel better with a little joke or story.

Deep down, however, the girl longed for home.

By the time June came along, she couldn't wait to pack her bags. So, on the last day of school, after lunch, Michelle joined in the farewell celebration with a gusto that was, at moments, marred by anxiety. Some of the boarders were going home that afternoon; others, within the following few days. She, however, still didn't know when she was going back. Her mother had not written yet to say who would come to get her.

As she was enjoying a piece of Sr. St. Jude's moist and rich gâteau au chocolat, Sr. St. Clara came up to her.

"Michelle, please come to see me at 4:30. I have something to tell you." She turned and quickly left the room.

"Okay," Michelle shouted gladly to the vanishing nun. She then went for a second helping and joined some of her friends who were talking about their plans for the summer.

Michelle always loved to have little conferences with Sister, so at 4:30 sharp she was eagerly knocking on the school room door.

"Come right in."

The girl turned the knob and walked in with a big smile. As soon as she saw Sister's face, however, the intuitive child's happy anticipation drained. She stopped.

"Come, come. . . Sit right here." Sister's smile did not match the message in her eyes.

Michelle dawdled over and sat down. "What's wrong, Sister. Why are you so sad?"

"I didn't realize I looked that sad," Sister answered, almost apologetically. She pinched her lips and paused for a moment. Then she got up and went to the child. "Michelle, I have some news for you. I'm afraid you won't like it."

The girl's fingers could not stay still as she waited for Sister to continue.

"We received a letter from your mother." She stopped for a deep breath. "She will soon have another baby, and she would like you to stay with us for the summer." Sister rubbed together her two cold hands.

Michelle was dazed, but within a second, she was up and screaming. "Why? Why does Maman have so many babies? Now I can't go home because of another baby! I'll bet it's another boy!" She turned and started to sob.

"Look at me, Michelle," Sister said softly. "It's *not* just about a new baby."

The girl looked straight at her. "Well that's what *you* just read! Maman said it's because of the baby."

"I know that's what she said, but it's really not *just* about the baby. Please believe me."

"Well, why then?"

Sister leaned toward the child. "Do you remember the day your grandmaman got very upset with your father--in the chicken coop?. . . Here's a hankie. Wipe your tears."

The girl dotted her eyes with the huge white handkerchief. "Yes. Grandmaman said she over-reacted."

"That's a big word, Michelle."

"Maman says that a lot to my big brothers when they get too excited."

"I see," Sister nodded. Then she paused for a moment, wondering how much she should tell the child. Finally, she said, "Your grandmaman was very upset because your father was about to hurt you again. That's why you were sent to us, and that's why your maman wants you to stay here now."

Michelle's face turned to confusion. "That's not true! My father was going to give me something that I like. He said so! Then Grandmaman came, and he left because *she* was so mad."

Sister took off her glasses and wiped them. She needed a minute to think. "I would *not lie* to you. Believe me, child, she *knew* that it was a bad surprise. That's why she was so angry. What did she tell you? "

"All she said was 'This is awful. It's awful!' Then we went into the house to see Maman."

"And what did *she* say?"

I don't know because I went to play with my toys. But I could hear them. Most of the time, they were talking very low, but sometimes one of them would scream some curse words. I really don't know why they were so angry."

"Well, I think they were right. He might have hurt you again. "

"But I was so glad, Sister. I know my father hits me when I'm bad, but this time he said I would really like his surprise. That means that he *loves* me even though I'm bad sometimes. I wanted it so much!"

"They'll tell you all about it when you grow up. Right now you wouldn't understand. Come here. You need a real, big hug."

Michelle pulled away. "I *know* it was a nice surprise."

Sister's heart pounded as she heard the girl's futile wish for a father's love. "Well, your maman loves you."

"I don't think so! How come I'm the only one she sends away? She never sends the boys to boarding school!"

Sister put her arms around the child and held her warmly. This time, Michelle hung on to her desperately.

When Michelle let go, Sister went to the class library and picked a book from the corner shelf. "Here's something for you to read. It's all about God and how much He loves us, how much He loves *you*."

Michelle took it, and when she saw the picture of God, the Father on the cover, she said, "He looks like a nice father, but he's old. He looks like a grandfather."

Sister chuckled. "God is spirit, Michelle. We can't take a picture of him. This image is just a way of showing us how kind and good He really is. You can bring the book to your room. And, by the way, believe me, the summer will go by very quickly because we will find all kinds of things for you to do around here with us."

Michelle's eyes widened. "With the Sisters? Inside the convent?"

"Of course. For instance, maybe you can help Sr. St. Jude make some of her luscious cakes. How about that?"

"Wow! I can't wait to tell my friends! They'll never believe me!"

The exhilaration, however, did not last very long.

A few days later, when all the girls were gone home and Sr. St. Clara had come to say goodnight to her, Michelle was all alone in the dorm filled with empty beds, strange noises that creaked and squeaked in the hollow room--and a gnawing homesickness in her heart. She cried for a while; then she tried to sleep, but she could not. Finally, she sat up in bed, lit the small bedside lamp and opened Sister's book.

Over and over again she looked at the images, especially the one of God, the Father smiling down at the world from a big cloud in heaven. Somehow she felt that He was smiling at her, and after a while she floated into the land of dreams. When she woke up the next morning, the lamp light was still on and the book was next to her under the thin, flannel summer blanket.

The next few days brought about a roller coaster of emotions. Although Michelle was very much occupied with routines that the Sisters had organized for her, she had moments of intense loneliness and ongoing emotional confusion, not only about her father, but also about her mother. She could not rid her mind of troublesome thoughts. *Maman never sent my brothers to boarding school! Why me? I think Papa had something nice for me. He said he did. Why did Sister say he did not?*

For years to come, these uncertainties, now taking root in her mind, would follow her like a bad dream that comes up when we least expect it.

"I'm Jean-Paul Dumont. . . but they call me JP."

By the middle of July, Michelle's disquieting emotions had moderated. The Sisters kept her so busy that the girl had less and less time to think of home. Her morning consisted mostly of Mass, chores, and periods set aside for reading and learning new things. In the afternoon, she would go out to play in the yard with her friends who lived in the house abutting the convent.

At the end of June, however, the family went away on vacation and Michelle was alone most of the time. When Sister St. Clara saw this, she asked one of the nuns to help the child start a small garden of her own in the back yard near a beaten, wooden fence that separated the property from the thicket. Michelle discovered that she loved gardening, and she spent much time taking care of her little space filled with blossoms and burgeoning flowers that had been transplanted from the main garden. Then one day, as she was watering her jardin, she heard a voice from behind the fence.

"Hey, can I come to play with you?"

Someone was peeking behind some broken boards in the fence. Surprised, Michelle marched over and saw that it was a boy. "Why do you wanna come to play with me?"

"My friends are gone on vacation, and I'm all alone," he said, rather glumly.

"Me too," Michelle admitted.

"So, let's play together. Can I come in?"

"I guess so," Michelle answered, "but how are you gonna come in?"

"No problem," the boy answered as he snapped a few boards out of the lower bar, rotated them upward, and wedged his way through the opening and into the yard. As he straightened up, he swished away a wavy tuft of black hair from his forehead, brushed some debris from his overalls, and eyed Michelle with the confidence of an athlete.

Michelle just stood there, totally amazed at the prowess of the handsome, eight-year old who had managed to sneak in. Then she wondered, "How did you know I was here?"

"I live near the pond on the other side," he answered as he pointed to the thicket. "I often play in the woods with my friends, but today I was alone, 'cause they're all gone. So, I went to climb trees by myself. That's when I saw you."

"Oh. . . Okay. What's your name?"

"I'm Jean Paul Dumont," he said proudly, "but they call me JP. What's *your* name?"

"Michelle Bellerose, and they call me Michelle," she said, as she imitated him.

JP laughed and slapped his thigh.

"You're funny," she said, and she started to mimic his gesture.

"So are you," he retorted, as they giggled unto tears.

And thus began an amazing friendship in a convent yard of Canada. No one could ever have imagined the course it would take and the effects it would have in the lives of these two youngsters.

"That's one for the books!"

Michelle was not allowed to leave the premises, so, almost every day, the boy sneaked through the fence and came to see her. They got along wonderfully, playing tag and hide-and-seek, or swinging into the sky, or seesawing thrillingly in the nearby school yard.

Unbeknown to Michelle, Sr. St. Veronique who was the first to see them together, had tried to stop the boy/girl friendship, but Sr. St. Clara had intervened. "Have a heart, Veronique, the kid's lonely. She needs a friend. What do you think he's going to do to her in front of our eyes. She's been told not to leave the yard, and she won't. You know that! Get with it. Times are changing. When I have a chance, I'll talk to her."

Sr. St. Veronique never said another word, and JP continued his furtive entries through the fence, never knowing that he could have come in through the front gate.

Then one day, when they were trying to think of a new game to play, JP proposed that they do something really outrageous. "Let's get out of here and go to the pond."

Michelle would have nothing to do with such an idea! That would be disobeying the Sisters! Never! On the other hand, she was getting bored, and it didn't take too much persuasion from JP for her to relent. So, she looked around to see if anyone was watching. When she saw that no one was in sight, they took off. Daringly and slyly they tip-toed to the end of the fence, crawled through the hole and ran into the thicket where JP led her to the path that would bring them to the pond.

As they tramped along the narrow clearing, Michelle picked up a large branch and was swishing it against the brush when JP interrupted her focus. "I hope my papa never finds out about this," he said with a tint of anxiety. "He'd be really mad."

"Me too," Michelle shivered as she thought about it. "You know what *my* father did?"

"No."

"He said he was going to give me something really, really nice, and he never did!" A mixture of anger and disappointment trembled in her voice.

"Why not?"

"I don't know. My grandmaman said that it was *not* something nice, but I don't believe her. Then Sister St. Clara said that my grandmaman is right. Now I don't know who to believe. Papa or them. I wanted it so much. But he never gave it to me. So maybe they're right."

"Why don't they tell you what it was?"

Michelle kicked a few rocks. "I don't know. It's like a big secret or something. I *hate* secrets!" They strolled in silence for a few minutes. "Sister said I'm too young; I wouldn't understand." She stopped. "I hate to be 'too young'." She pointed her forefinger at JP. "When I grow up, I'll find out, and I'll tell you about it."

JP's eyes almost popped out. "You will?"

"Of course. You're my friend, aren't you?" They started off again. "Sister gave me a nice book with the picture of God, the Father. Did you ever see him?"

"No. Never heard of him."

"Well, he's kind of old. He has white hair, a white beard and a nice smile. He looks like a grandfather, but she says he's not a grandfather. He's God, the Father and He loves us all."

"Really?" JP exclaimed with curiosity.

"*Everyone!* That's what Sister said. I sure would like to meet him one day."

"Gee, that would be fun," JP commented, as they both started skipping toward the water that was now in their sight.

Suddenly, Michelle stopped. "Look! Over there!" she cried excitedly and pointed to a man sitting on a wooden bench near the huge, tall clock that was the distinguishing mark of the small park. He was watching a bunch of children playing in the water.

Jean Paul turned quickly. "Who? Where?"

"Right there!" she said, as she grabbed his hand and started running.

At the unexpected tug JP lost his balance and fell down, but not for long. Michelle heaved him upward, and off they went.

As they got closer to the man, Michelle halted. She looked straight at JP. "Could it be?"

JP shrugged. "Be what?"

"Never mind," she said as she went right up to the man and stood in awe before him.

He looked at her staring at him and finally said, "What are you looking at, kid?"

"Are you God?" Michelle asked hesitantly.

"What?" the man's eyes circled wide in surprise.

Michelle repeated, "Are you God?"

The man started to laugh, as he tapped himself on the lap. "Me? God? Wow! That's one for the books!"

"Well. . are you?" she asked impatiently.

"Why do you think I'm God?" he chuckled.

Michelle answered, "You've got long white hair and a big white beard. That's what God, the Father looks like. We're looking for him."

"And that's what Santa Claus looks like, too!" he responded, as a laugh from deep in the belly shook his whole body. "Well, at least I look like two *good* persons," he continued. "That's more than I could ever dream of since I've been out of jail. Why are you looking for God?"

"Because He's really, really a good Father," the girl answered. "Sister says that He knows me and loves me. So, I want to know him, too."

"Well, kiddo, it sure would have been nice to have that God around when I was your age. I wish you luck, though. As for me, it's a little late to be looking for him. What's your name?"

"Michelle."

"Hmm... And what's yours?" he asked, as he turned towards the boy.

"Jean Paul Larivière," the boy answered proudly, and immediately pointed to Michelle. "She's Michelle *Bellerose!*"

"Sounds good," the stranger noted. He leaned forward, placed his elbow on his lap and restlessly twitched his beard. "I'm just visiting here, so I don't know much French. Do those names mean anything?"

"His name means 'the river' and mine means 'pretty rose'," Michelle responded immediately.

"Hmm. . . interesting." The children's enthusiasm and simplicity brought a twinkle to his narrow, blue eyes, and he grinned.

"What's *your* name?" Jean Paul inquired.

"Ivan."

JP's face wrinkled curiously. "That's a strange name."

"Not where I come from," the man replied, as he relaxed and stretched his legs.

Then a screeching cry came from the water. "Help! Help!" Everyone started running toward the small beach.

"Looks like he's drowning!" the man said as he jumped up and ran to the water's edge. Within seconds he had taken off his shoes and was swimming to the child who had gone too far out."

Although he had not swum in years and was having difficulty breathing, Ivan seemed to draw from an unexpected energy and got to the child just as he was going down again. He then managed to get a solid hold of the boy, and after incredible efforts he pulled him to shore.

Michelle and JP watched in horror from afar as groups of children and adults congregated around the exhausted old man and the seemingly lifeless body. Immediately a woman, who, they later found out was a nurse, ran to the victim and Ivan stepped away as she yelled, "Someone call for an ambulance." Then she knelt and bent over the boy. After what seemed like hours, but before the ambulance arrived, she stood and announced enthusiastically, "He'll be okay! This man saved his life!"

As the crowd cheered and clapped thunderously, Ivan got up and trudged slowly back to the bench.

When he sat down, his face was almost as white as his hair.

Michelle, who was now sitting on the grass, looked at him with childlike astonishment. "You are like God," she said. "You saved him!"

At that moment, the chimes in the clock rang and JP pulled Michelle's hand. "Come on. It's three o'clock. We'd better go back to the convent. The Sisters will be looking for you!"

Michelle jumped up. "Oh no! Bye, Mr. Ivan," she hollered as they took off and ran so fast that her long hair floated behind as if carried by the wind.

She had just crawled back through the fence and was trying to slow down her heavy breathing when she heard Sr. St. Clara.

"Michelle! Michelle! It's time to come in."

Whew! That was a close call! She thought as she waved good-bye to JP and ran to the convent.

By night time, Michelle was exhausted. The afternoon's clandestine adventure had left its mark on her and as soon as she went to bed she was out of this world and into the land of happy dreams.

Had she known what awaited her the next day, she would have had a nightmare.

"We'll always be friends, won't we?"

The next day, as Michelle watched JP come through the fence, suddenly, she felt a great uneasiness. He looked sad and pale. "What's the matter?"

"I can't stay," he blurted out, "and I won't be able to come anymore."

Michelle's heart almost stopped. "Why?"

"My dad can't find work in Canada, so we have to go far away."

Still stunned, she asked, "How far away?"

He shrugged. "All he said was, 'somewhere in the states'."

"But you're my best friend," Michelle said, "What'll I do?"

"You're my best friend, too," the boy said, as he went close to her. "I don't wanna go, but I have to." He started to cry and she put her arms around him. They hugged. "We'll always be friends, won't we?" he said plaintively.

Tears were now flowing freely down the girl's cheeks. "Yes. We'll always be friends," she said sobbingly. "Can't you stay here for a while?"

"No. My father thinks I've been going to the park. He'll come look for me if I don't go back soon. I have to go."

He turned, and she stood staring as he walked away and disappeared behind the fence.

For the second time in just a few weeks, a sense of emptiness caused her such deep pain that all she wanted to do was run and run and run. . .

Prophetic thoughts indeed, for she, also, was about to move again!

"Why can't I go home?"

Two days later, Sr. St. Clara told Michelle that she had received a letter from her mother. The girl was pleasantly surprised since Marie, who had left school at fourteen, was very self-conscious about her writing skills and she had only written two very short notes since the previous September. As usual, this was brief. Sister read it to the girl whose face was filled with glad expectation.

My dear Michelle   *July 28, 1948*

I hope you are well. Aunt Lena will come to get you very soon to bring you to live with her in New Hampshire. She will take good care of you. I'm sure you will be happy there.

Your new brother, Leon, is very sick. Please pray for him. Everything else is fine.

Love,

Maman

Michelle became hysterical. "I don't want to go to Aunt Lena. I want to go home!"

Sister hugged her. "Shh. . . It's okay. You'll see. Everything will be okay."

"Why can't I go home?" Michelle pleaded. "I could help my maman, but she doesn't want me!"

Sister Clara bit her lips and decided to ignore the last remark. "Your aunt must love you very much to bring you home with her. I heard that she's a very nice person."

"I don't know. I only saw her one time," Michelle answered. "She gave me some candy that she made."

"Well, there you are. Any aunt who would make candy especially for her little niece must be a very good aunt, indeed. Besides, you won't be there for a very long time. One day you'll go back home. In the meantime, I'm told that your aunt lives near a fine school where you'll make new friends. I'm sure you'll have a lot of fun."

The girl wasn't convinced, but she calmed down and kept staring at the floor.

Then Sister spoke softly. "Michelle, remember what your mother told you about finding good things in life, even when everything seems to go wrong?"

A weak "yes" escaped Michelle's lips.

"Well, you've done that before and you can surely do it again. Give it a try, okay? Now what nice things could happen at Aunt Lena's?"

Michelle lifted her head and started to imagine. "Maybe she'll show me how to make that good candy; maybe I'll have some nice new friends; maybe my aunt will buy me roller skates. . . Maybe she'll bring me back home."

CHAPTER 3

They walked out. . . into a completely different world.

By the time Aunt Lena arrived two days later, Michelle was waiting with much anxiety. When she saw the heavy-set woman with a wide-brimmed purple hat covering most of her tightly-permed hair, the girl tried to remember her, but the memory was very vague.

A few seconds later, the bell rang and when Sister opened the door, Lena walked in confidently, said "Good afternoon" to the nuns who were gathering to say farewell to Michelle, and went straight to the girl. "My, how you've grown!" she exclaimed heartily, as she hugged her niece. "I'm so glad you'll be coming to live with me."

She then turned to the gathering. "After four years of marriage, my husband died and left me childless." She sent a kiss to Michelle--and words to the Sisters, "It'll be a joy to have her around."

Sister St. Clara looked fondly at Michelle whose dark, wistful eyes and forced smile seemed to be pleading for some kind of familiar security. "We'll miss her, but we're glad she'll be in a safe and loving home," she said solicitously, as she hugged her little protégé who did not seem to want to let her go.

After a few minutes of light gossip and gabbing, Lena took Michelle's hand. "It's time to leave now."

The girl said a tearful good-by to the nuns and went to hug Sister St. Clara again.

Then, Lena picked up the suitcase and they walked out the door, into a completely different world.

As they approached the big car, Michelle was surprised to see a man in the driver's seat. When he saw them coming, he got out and came to open the doors for them. After greeting Michelle with "Hello, young lady", he opened the back door and heaved her suitcase to the opposite end of the seat. Michelle hopped in and wiggled in so far back that her feet did not even touch the floor. Then she watched as the man helped Lena get into her seat, carefully closed her door and returned to his place at the wheel. Once settled in, he took off the brown fedora that had hidden his wavy blond hair, and he switched on the ignition.

As the car took off, Lena turned around. "Michelle, this is Bozo, my boyfriend."

Without looking behind, Bozo waved his right hand, immediately returned it to the wheel, and focused on the road that started them on their way back to the United States.

Michelle looked at him suspiciously, but said nothing. After a few moments, however, her curiosity won. She leaned forward and whispered, to Lena, "His name is Bozo?"

In front, they both heard her and started to laugh. "That's not my real name," the man said, as he glanced in the rear-view mirror. "Do you think that I look like a bozo?"

Michelle giggled. "I don't know. What does a bozo look like?"

"Like anything you want!" he answered back. "When I was a boy they gave me that nickname because I used to make stupid remarks--so they say. But I don't believe them, of course. And neither should you!"

"Did you hear that, Michelle? He's denying it. Just wait. Those remarks are *not* restricted to his boyhood.

You'll soon see and *hear* what I mean." Lena's big hat jumped up and down as she and Bozo started giggling like kids.

Michelle wasn't sure what she meant, but their giggling was so contagious that she soon joined in their laughter.

After a few other back-and-forth comments, Bozo and Lena were almost in guffaws and Michelle was on the verge of tears. For once, they were happy tears.

Finally, the merriment diminished and Lena gave Michelle her first rule. "Just remember, sweetheart, we never call him 'Bozo' in public. Never, ever! His real name is Leo Lavigne, and he's far from being stupid. In fact, I think he's the smartest man in town. He even finished high school and took some college courses in accounting. Isn't that great!"

"Yes," Michelle answered politely, but in reality, she was not impressed because completing high school or going to college didn't mean much to her family.

Then Lena proudly announced her own feat. "I got a high-school diploma, too. Did you know that? What a pleasure it was to get *that* piece of paper! It didn't come easily, though. I worked very hard to get it."

That revelation didn't particularly interest Michelle either. However, she could feel her aunt's elation, so she looked straight at her and said, "Wow."

"You'll get one, too," Aunt Lena promised her. "It's the only way to get a good job and become an independent woman. Look at me. I'd never be working in a bank without it."

Michelle said "Wow" again. Then she turned to look out the window and watch the farmlands stream by as the car sped toward the "states" and into a life that she could only have dreamed of.

Eight hours later they arrived in Oakton, a small town in southern New Hampshire that was filled with ethnic neighborhoods populated by immigrants from Canada and European countries who came looking for work. It was not uncommon for most of them to have very large families, so the men, who were the wage earners, put in long and arduous labor in the mills to support their brood. Even the children had to help. By the time they reached fourteen or fifteen, they also went to work in the factories. Surely, they had no time to think of education.

Neither did the women who remained at home. They worked from dawn to night preparing meals, changing diapers, intervening in sibling quarrels, washing laundry in tubs or machines with wringers, sewing and altering clothes, mending socks, and doing a multitude of other chores that left them exhausted by the time they went to bed very late at night. "Bread on the table", not "head in the books", was the common goal of most of the families.

Lena, however, had ideas of her own. When her husband died and left her childless, she was depressed and disconsolate, but she did not stay down for long. One day, alone at the kitchen table, she sobbed herself dry. Wiping the last salty tear from her lip, she stood up and asserted to herself that she would have a life again. During that evening, her thoughts traveled to many places and many things, and her imagination fed her with possibilities she had never imagined.

So, although her husband had a generous life insurance, she decided to return to work, but not in a mill. *No more of that!* She thought. *Never again!*

A few days later, feeling like a new woman, she enrolled in a relatively young program called GED. When she finally got the certificate, she hung it in the living room, safely secured in an expensive frame. Then, all alone, she celebrated with champagne. Under her firm grip, the bottle fired its cork, the liquor splashed out and Lena filled her high-stemmed glass. "Three cheers!" she exclaimed as she swung the glass in the air, and kissed her certificate. She felt like Wonder Woman.

The next day she went looking for an office job. That's what she had always dreamed of: a professional-type job, a desk of her own, and a pleasant, quiet environment. Within a week, she was hired as a teller at the Union Savings in the downtown district. She had no desk of her own, of course, but two out of three wishes wasn't so bad, and she was sure that eventually she *would* get the third.

That's where she met Leo. He had worked his way up to Head Bookkeeper in the hospital finance department and it was his job to bring certain weekly deposits to the bank. The first time that Lena waited on him, he was smitten. "Love at first sight" he called it, and he began to devise strategies to end up at her window all the time.

She, on the other hand, was not interested in him or his trivial, home-made remarks, and after his fourth success at landing at her station for service, she tried to shift him to other tellers. They were not too cooperative, however, because word had gotten around that Leo seemed to be more than attracted to Lena, and they had started to place bets on the outcome.

Then it happened. Leo got daring and asked her for a date. She refused, of course. But Leo considered this nothing more than a common situational challenge. So he tried the next week, and the next, and. . .

Finally, she decided that the best way to settle this was to accept to go to dinner with him and make it so unpleasant that he would never bother her again.

So on the following Saturday, she had a bagful of "misbehaviors" (like talking very loud in the restaurant or spilling expensive wine on the floor) ready to launch as opportune moments showed up. She waited for Leo with a certain glee.

He arrived at 7 p.m. sharp with a fabulous corsage of red roses, pinned it on her and then chauffeured her to a posh restaurant in Keene, where they dined and danced until closing time.

When she returned home that night, she was in shock! The whole evening, as well as Leo, had been so wonderful that she didn't even have time to think about her sabotage!

So, although it was very late, she was not tired at all, and she sat in her favorite armchair wondering how she could have misjudged him so much! Beyond his occasional cockeyed comments, he was caring, ambitious, intelligent, thoughtful, and, a perfect gentleman. Better yet, he was a wonderful dancer--a rarity in the crowds that she had frequented. As for looks, he wasn't a magazine model, but he had interesting blue eyes, unblemished skin and real teeth that could have passed for high-quality dentures.

Now, three years had gone by since that first date, and they had slipped into an exclusive, but only friendly relationship. Leo wanted to get married, but Lena would have none of it.

"I'll never be able to love another man" was her repeated and *very faint* response. But her relish of independence came through like a scream, and Leo heard it loud and clear. He was determined, however, to stay in the race.

Lena, of course, had reasons to enjoy her freedom. During those three years, she had been promoted and had finally earned the pleasure of sitting at her own desk. Now she was a loan supervisor and she thoroughly enjoyed the amenities of the steps up the ladder: new challenges, new friends and new status. In this situation, which she considered to be enviable, she could well afford to take in Michelle and bring her up to become a fine, young woman.

A worthy goal, indeed, but one that would split Michelle in two.

Part of the "inner circle"

Once more, Michelle adapted well to her new life.

Lena enrolled her in a private Catholic school, bought her clothes in Boston boutiques, and exposed her to what she called "the classier things in life", including theater and classical music. In fact, if ever there was a conflict between a popular, highly-raved movie and a symphony concert, the movie got left behind--even when Lena would have preferred to go to the "silver screen." She was always ready to sacrifice the common flick for the upscale concerts that sometimes even bored her. Leo, on the other hand, was enraptured by the music, and Michelle grew to love it so much that she decided to take piano lessons.

Most of all, however, Lena made sure that Michelle would associate only with the elite in the area and, within a few months, her niece had become part of an "inner circle" of friends from some of the more prominent families around.

There was nothing wanting in Michelle's life. Yet, in quiet times, her heart would reach for home, and she would cry silently, wishing that her mother would love her and hoping that her father did.

She never told her aunt, but how often she would wait for the mailman to come! Maybe he would bring a letter from her mother asking her to come back home. . . Maybe he would deliver the nice surprise that her father had promised. . . Maybe. . .

The surprise from her father came all right, but it surely was not what Michelle was expecting.

"Who started that rumor?"

A few years passed, and one day Michelle was at her best friend Gloria's highfalutin birthday party when, after the rest of the guests had left, the girls in the "inner circle" got involved in private, personal chatter.

One of them started to complain about her mother. "She's always nagging me," Laura lamented, as she crunched a maxi pretzel, "but I just let it go over my head."

"You should be glad that's all she does," Maryanne said, as she threw an M&M into her open mouth. "My mother screams all the time. Sometimes I feel like telling her to shut up."

"That wouldn't be very nice," timorous Terry dared to say, as she delicately picked a pretzel.

"I could care less about 'nice'," Maryanne confessed. "I just don't want to get grounded."

"I know how to fix your problem," jolly Jeannette sounded off. "Just get ear plugs."

When the giggling stopped, Laura, who had been crackling chips, grabbed another handful and turned to Michelle. "What about *your* mother?" she asked, "You never talk about her."

Terry put her finger to her lips and leaned toward Laura. "Shh. . . Her mother's dead. Don't you know that?"

Michelle heard her and jumped up. "My mother's *not* dead!" she said with an affirmation that made the table tremble.

"I'm sorry. I thought she was." Terry's face flushed with embarrassment. "That's what I heard."

"Well, you heard wrong! Who started that rumor?"

"I don't know," Terry was now as pale as the cream soda she held in her hand.

"Well, how come you live with your aunt?" Jeannette asked, as she poured more Kool Aid into her glass.

For a moment Michelle didn't know what to answer. Then she blurted out, "So that I could come to school here. My mother says it's one of the finest schools, and she wants me to get the finest education. That's why." She dropped back into the sofa, scooped up some M&Ms, and abruptly changed the subject. "I'd like to hear that Bing Crosby record again."

Jeannette, the ice cutter, called out, "Gladly!" She jumped up to get the record. "You all know how much I love Bing Crosby!" she announced in sing-song

As the crooner's mellow voice filled the room with "The Bells of St. Mary", the girls started to sing along, and for the rest of the evening the conversation was about anything and everything--except mothers.

Michelle tried to join them, but she couldn't even remember the words. Anxiety now had her in its grip.

Maryanne noticed the girl's troubled countenance and she approached her. "What's wrong?"

Michelle looked at her watch. She wanted to go home, but it would be at least another half hour before her aunt would come for her. "Nothing. I'm just tired."

"Well, maybe you just had too much birthday cake." Maryanne turned away and started to swing and swirl with a polka that had just begun.

Michelle hardly said a word for the rest of the evening.

"Because it's none of their business!"

Finally, as the clock struck nine, Lena arrived. Punctuality was almost an obsession with her, and though it irritated Michelle at times, tonight the girl was ready to bless her for being on time.

When they got into the car, the first thing she asked was, "Is Maman dead?"

"My heavens! Why do you ask that?" Lena responded, as she started the vehicle. The question stunned her so much that she moved the clutch at the wrong time, and they both winced, as a grinding noise beat on their ear drums.

"Of course she's not dead," Lena said, as she made a second attempt at starting her Hudson. "Why do you ask that?"

When Michelle told her what had happened, Lena just shrugged it off. "If something had happened to your mother, someone would have called us. Don't worry. Your mother's fine."

"But why did Terry think that?"

"Must be because we never discuss our family with outsiders. Whatever happens in the family, *stays in* the family. You've heard that often enough."

"But why hide? Maman didn't do anything wrong."

"Michelle, it's not about right and wrong. All family matters are private. That's all!"

Michelle still could not understand. "Well, if I don't say anything about my mother, why do the others talk about her? They don't even know her!"

Lena sighed heavily. "Well, I guess when people don't know the facts, they start making up stories. That's what happened tonight."

"If that's the case, why *don't* we talk about my family?" the bewildered girl asked.

"Because it's none of their business!" Lena almost growled as the front tire rolled over the curb and bounced back onto the driveway asphalt. Michelle slid on the seat and her purse fell off her lap. As she bent to pick it up, the car stopped abruptly, and she bumped her head on the dashboard, but she hardly noticed what was happening: her focus was still on her mother.

She said nothing until they were taking off their coats in the front hallway. "If Maman's alive, why doesn't she answer the letter that I sent her? Are you sure she's not dead?"

"I'm 100% sure, Michelle. She never writes a lot. You know that! The woman is just too busy! I know it's hard for you to understand, but your mother must work from dawn to the time she goes to bed--if she has time for that! I'm sure she loves you very much, but she just doesn't have time to write."

Michelle's face started a pouting session. "She just likes the boys more than me."

"I don't want to hear that anymore!" the woman snapped. "Your mother's having a hard time because she chose to marry into low life instead of going to school. At fourteen she quit school and went to work in a mill. Then, when she was old enough, she quit that and became a waitress in a club. The patrons liked her, and she liked them. Unfortunately, she liked one *too much.* That was your father. He promised her all kinds of things, and one day he came in with a diamond ring--wherever he may have gotten it. Probably was stolen. Anyhow, that did it! She was hooked."

"What do you mean?" Michelle winced as she tried to understand.

"She got married! I was only ten at the time. But I remember clearly that no one in our family liked El, and they tried to stop the marriage. But she was blind and hardheaded, and they eloped. Didn't even get married in church! My parents were heartbroken, and I thought they would never speak to her again. But, later on they did. We all did--which didn't stop us from being heartbroken at the stupid choice she made."

"I don't care. I love my mother--and my father, too!"

Lena took her in her arms. "That's okay, dear. Your mother's a good woman who loves you very much. I love her, too, even though I get upset with her at times. When she has time to write, she will. And better yet, when you're a little older, we'll even go see her. Okay?"

The girl sniffled a bit. "How old will I have to be?"

"Maybe when you're sixteen or so. Okay?"

"But I'm only ten years old. That's a long time!"

"I know, but it will come fast. You'll see."

Michelle was not convinced. Lena had attempted to put salve on the situation, but it had not worked. To Michelle, "sixteen" might as well have been "sixty".

"It would be a shame to say 'no' now."

Three years later Leo was almost dancing on the table. Lena had finally said "Yes".

The next day he was passing out cigars, as men did when a baby was born. When Lena found out, she was furious. "Don't you do that!" she shrieked, "They'll think I'm pregnant!"

"How could they think that?" he bantered, "You're thirty-one years old. Already over the hill!" He winked at Michelle who was laughing heartily.

"You son-of-a-gun!" Lena dove into him and ended up in his arms.

Michelle left the room.

They got married in a private event. Contrary to the huge, pretentious affairs that made Lena such a popular hostess, her second marriage was a quiet ceremony before a priest, with only a few relatives and very close friends in attendance.

Now thirteen, Michelle was the junior bridesmaid and she never forgot what Leo. . . er, Bozo. . . did at the most solemn part of the ritual. When the time came to say "I do", he looked straight at the priest and whispered, "Almost eight years I've been waiting for this. It would be a shame to say 'no' now. Right?" Then he turned, smiled widely at Lena, and said "You bet I do" loud enough for all to hear.

The reception was in a small, reserved room at the elegant Lucinda's Fine Dining restaurant in a Keene suburb. A piano player, violinist and fiddler provided a combination of soft, old-time melodies and foot-tapping, heart-rushing Canadian music for the affair. At the end of the final dance where Leo literally swept Lena off her feet by whirling her around and right off the floor during a quadrille, he remained in the center of the floor, held her hand and made an announcement. "The pearl necklace that I gave you is not the only gift I bought."

Lena's eyebrows arched high above her widening eyes.

"As of yesterday we own a brand new seven-room bungalow. . . Lena, I'll never forget the look on your face right now!" Then he signaled Michelle to join them.

Everyone cheered and clapped, and as Michelle walked up to join the couple, Leo heartily proclaimed, "And we'll all be happy there for a long, long time."

Everyone cheered and wished them well.

In less than two years, however, their dream life was crumbled by a simple telephone call.

Jeannette's voice was curt and cold.

By the time she was fifteen, Michelle had grown into a poised and happy teenager. She was doing extra well in school and in her piano studies, and she was already planning to be the very first one in her whole family to go to college.

A month before her sixteenth birthday, she sat down to make a list of the people she would invite to her party. The "inner circle", of course would be at the top of the list. Terry had moved away, however, and Michelle could not find her new address, so she made some phone calls. Neither Gloria nor Maryanne were home. Finally she called Jeannette and Michelle's comfortable world shattered like broken glass.

"Oh, it's you," Jeannette's voice was curt and cold.

Michelle was so startled that, for a moment, she was speechless. Jeannette was the only one in the "circle" who never seemed to have bad days. She was happy-go-lucky, friendly and could warm up a freezer. Finally Michelle said, "Yes, it's me. I need some information."

Silence. . . "Jeannette, are you there?"

"Yes. I'm sorry, Michelle, but we can't be friends anymore."

"Why? Did I do something to hurt you?"

"No. But I know it now. In fact, we all know it."

"Know what?"

"How many 'Elphège Bellerose' can there be in a town as small as Mapleview, Vermont?"

"I don't know. Why are you asking that?"

"That's your father's name, isn't it?"

"Yes. So what!"

"Oh, come on. You know darned well. I can see why you didn't want to talk about it, though."

Michelle leaned against the wall for support. "Jeannette, I have no idea what you're talking about."

"Your father's in prison, and you don't know it! That's ridiculous," Jeannette hollered.

Michelle dropped the handset. As she bent to retrieve it, her legs jelloed, and she sat on the floor. "Is this another one of those crazy rumors? Who told you that?"

"Uncle Bill. Last year, he asked, and you told him your father's name. Remember? Anyhow, now my uncle's a guard at the State prison, and was he ever surprised when he was assigned to lead an 'Elphège Bellerose' to his cell. And when he found out that he *really* was your father! Well, that did it! So, we can't be friends anymore." She hung up.

Michelle got up, slammed the phone, and gravitated to the sofa where she lay down and was in such a daze that she could neither think nor move. After a while, the conversation returned to haunt her. *Is that a rumor? Or is it true?*

"Why didn't you tell me?"

Two hours later, Lena came home. Entering by the back door, she assumed that Michelle was somewhere within ear-reach and she hollered, "Hi." Hearing no response and noticing that nothing in the kitchen had been disturbed, she strolled into the living room. "You haven't started supper yet?"

Then she saw Michelle sitting on the edge of the sofa, elbows on her knees and face in her hands. "What's wrong?"

The girl didn't even look up. "Why didn't you tell me?"

"Tell you what?"

"My father's in prison and you didn't even tell me!" the girl exploded. "And what the hell did he do?"

Lena raised both her hands. "Whoa, there! I don't know anything about that. Keep "hell" out of your conversation and tell me what's going on? Who said that? Will they ever stop those damned rumors!" she sat down next to Michelle and took her hand.

When Michelle told her about Jeannette, Lena's elbow plopped on the arm rest and her hand went up to cup her face. For a moment, she looked helpless. Michelle had never seen her aunt so limp and she felt scared.

It did not last long, however. Within a few minutes, Lena's body rose against the back cushions, her head straightened up, and her face took on the determination of an Olympic champ. Aunt Lena was back! "There's only one way to find out if this is true or not. Surely my mother must know." She sprang up to go to the phone. A few minutes later, Cecile confirmed the news.

Lena's teeth clacked as her face contorted. "Why didn't you call me? Why did we have to find out from someone else? How do you think Michelle feels now?"

"He's only there for a few months," the grandmother explained. "He started a fight in Joe's Café and hurt someone. We didn't want to upset you or Michelle with something like this. How did I know it would get to New Hampshire?"

"Well, it did, and it's just awful! Now Jeannette doesn't want to be friends with Michelle anymore. I guess that goes for the others, too. You know how people are around here! If we had known, maybe we could have done something to prevent this. It's just awful!"

"I'm so sorry. Wait, I have to get a hankie." After auditioning a few nose blows, she returned to the phone. "Please tell Michelle that I am *so* sorry. I love her so much. You know I would never want to do something to hurt her."

"Okay, I'll tell her. I just don't know what will happen now! I'll talk to you later. Bye."

"Wait!" the mother shouted. "Wait. I just thought of something."

What is it? I have to go. I need time to think!" Lena almost bellowed.

"Well, now that El is away, maybe it's a good time for Michelle to go visit her mother."

"Oh, no! No!" Lena's eyes rolled up and swirled around the ceiling.

"Listen, Lena. The girl hardly knows her mother. She hasn't seen her in years, and I'll bet she'd like to go see her."

"I don't think so!" Lena said with loaded emphasis.

"I know you, Lena--more than you think," her mother started. "Don't keep her away from her mother. Michelle is old enough to go back home for a visit and now the coast is clear. It won't be for long. He's been in prison for a month already. You *have* to bring her. At least talk to her about it. Ask her. If you don't, Lena, *I will*."

"Okay, okay. I'll think about it," Lena answered unenthusiastically and closed the phone. Plunk!

Out of the question! No way am I telling her, or bringing her.

It's going to be another long night, he thought.

When Michelle came home from school the next day, Lena knew that the worst had happened. Word about her father had really spread, and her friends had turned from being welcoming to polite. After making a few inquiries, she realized that it was useless to send out invitations to her "Sweet Sixteen Party" because no one would come.

When she told Lena, Michelle's eyes filled with tears, but she quickly brushed them away. "This, too will pass. Isn't that what you always tell me," she said to Lena.

"It will. You'll see. Nothing on this earth lasts forever." *Besides, I'll see to it that it doesn't.*

Then the girl's eyes shifted pleadingly to Lena's. "What about my mother? What is she going to do with my father gone? Where will she get money? Do you think my brothers are helping her?"

"He's away for only a few months, dear," Lena answered, as she turned her gaze away from the girl. "I'm sure your mother will be fine."

"How do you know? I want to go see her. You said I could go see her when I'm sixteen. I remember!"

"We'll go one day, Michelle--as soon as we can." Lena tried to sound reassuring.

"I'm almost sixteen! I want to go *now*. You promised!"

"Now is *not* a good time," Lena answered. "Let's talk about other things--nice things--like what can we do for your birthday."

Michelle's voice took a leap. "I don't care about my birthday anymore. I don't want anything. Nothing! Except to go see my mother! You promised!" She flung her books over her shoulder and ran up to her room.

Lena headed for the coffee can. Once the brewing got underway, she sat down to wait for Leo who was working late that day.

By the time he came home at ten, she was very agitated and working on emptying the coffee pot that was keeping her company.

As he hung his coat on the rack, Lena's words bounced in and out of his ears. By the time he sat near her, he knew three things: Elphège was in prison, Michelle wanted to go see her mother, and Lena's biggest problem was that she did not want to bring her.

"It's such a big mess," the woman rattled on, as she yanked a grape from its stem and put it in her mouth. "I have enough problems trying to ease the situation around here without having to bring Michelle to see her mother. Right?"

Leo thought it over and reached for the java that was left in the pot. This was a moment for few words. "Mess, messy and messier," he finally said.

"Your homemade nonsense again," Lena blurted out, "What are you talking about?"

"That's all you'll do by refusing her. Can't you see that?" He took a large gulp of the coffee and heaved a sigh.

"No. That will only make it worse." She got up to rinse the percolator and make fresh coffee.

"You're right. It'll be a *worse* mess. That's what I just said. Mess, messy, messier."

"This isn't funny, Bozo. Michelle is still too young."

"Too young for what? To see her mother? You don't have much respect for your sister, do you?"

"Of course I respect her."

"Well, what is it then? You afraid the girl will like her more than you?"

"Come on, Leo. That was uncalled for!"

"Well then, what is it?" He eyed her.

Lena closed her eyes. For a long time, neither said a word. Then she got up. "Take care of the coffee. I'm going to bed," she told him in a tone that only Leo would understand.

The coffee was percolating wildly, so he shut the gas and took the pot off the burner. *I guess it's going to be another long night*, he pondered, as he filled his cup again. Then he thought of Michelle--and his heart ached.

The next morning, when Michelle came down for breakfast, Lena and Leo were waiting for her. The night had been restless and troubling for Lena, but it had also given her time to think more reasonably. Now, very reluctantly, she had decided to listen to her husband.

"One more day and you'll be sixteen years old!" Leo announced. "I can't believe how fast time goes."

"Ya," was all that the girl uttered, as her eyes followed the Cheerios she had started to pour in her bowl.

Slipping the 'happy clown' features over her face, Lena said to Michelle," We have a very special birthday present for you. You'll really love it."

Michelle shrugged and slid the spoon into her cereal.

"It's something you've been wanting for a long time," Leo added. He leaned forward and looked at her in the eyes. "You know--like as long as you've been wanting me to stop making bozo remarks."

"I never said that!"

"But you've thought of it!" He winked at Lena.

Michelle looked straight at him. "That's not true. You don't know my thoughts!" She picked up her orange juice.

"I know some of them," he responded. "I know that you've been longing to go see your mother, so we're bringing you to Mapleview for your birthday."

Michelle dropped her juice glass into her cereal which suddenly changed to the color of Sunkist oranges.

"Now is that a way to say 'thank you'," Leo asked Lena.

She laughed, but inside her thoughts were rumbling. *It's been ten years. . . I wonder what it will be like. Maybe I'll wish we would never have gone.*

CHAPTER 4

The house was not as she remembered it.

On January 22, 1956 Michelle woke up early. She had left the window shade rolled up and the rays of the rising sun that streamed onto her bed energized the lightness in her heart. She got up quickly and as she started to dress, the smell of bacon and eggs being expertly prepared by Lena reached her nostrils and her stomach. Within a few minutes, she was seated at the breakfast table, waiting for Leo to come in. He had gone out to scrape the ice off his windshield and get the car ready for the trip.

Two hours later, they were on their way to visit her mother. An atmosphere of mixed emotions could be felt in the confines of the car, and very few words were spoken. Leo kept his focus on the road and drove steadfastly northward on the ride to her home. It had snowed a few days before and though the main routes had been plowed, the curvy up hills and down hills in the mountain area were still difficult and somewhat dangerous to maneuver.

On some of the mountain roads where they were so close to the edge that they could almost look down thousands of feet, Michelle's stomach took a queasy dip and Lena gripped her big pocketbook fiercely, as if it would protect her if the car took a dive down a ravine.

Most of the trip, however, was actually awesome, as they enjoyed the fabulous mountain landscapes of Vermont. Michelle, especially, had never seen such splendid snow-patched mountains and she thought that one day she might become a painter and return to this area to immortalize them on canvas.

Four hours later, Leo announced that they had just crossed into Mapleview.

Michelle could almost hear her heartbeat. Then, when she saw the "Martin Street" sign, her whole body became alert to everything that she could see and hear. She hardly recognized the area. Had it changed that much? Or had she been so young when she left that now she could not remember what it looked like? Then the familiar sign of "Bellini's Market" came into view. "Oh look! That's where I used to go on errands for my mother," she cried out. "Mr. Bellini always gave me a lollipop."

"That was a lulu thing to do," Leo said, as he carefully wove the car around a curve.

"There goes Bozo again," Michelle said to Lena. "I never heard that one before."

"That's because he never said that before," Lena laughed. "What are you talking about---Bozo?"

"It was a *nice* thing for him to do," Leo answered nonchalantly. "Were the lollipops good?"

"You bet. I made sure they were all gone before I got home. That's why I walked back so slowly."

"Shame on you, for not wanting to share with your brothers," Lena jested.

"Divide my lollipop among four boys and me! No one would have enough to enjoy it!"

"Wise, even at that age, hey!" Leo cast a glance at Michelle, via the rear-view mirror.

Then the car stopped. "Here we are, ladies: Sixty-four Martin Street!"

Michelle gulped. The house was not as she remembered it. Only ten years had gone by, but in contrast with the gleaming patches of snow on the roof, the sparkling icicles along the gutters, and the layers of pure white snow on the ground, the house seemed dull, and its façade looked as if it had gone through an uneven potato peeler. The front porch was tilting at one end, the wooden steps seemed ready to give way before the slightest weight, and the asphalt path, which had been shoveled, showed cracks waiting to be filled with weeds in the spring.

Lena and Leo looked at one another and, for a moment, said nothing.

Within a few seconds, Michelle's mother came running out of the house and the girl's heart pounded as she saw the skinny woman rush toward them. Michelle was so excited that she had trouble finding the handle and opened the door just as Marie reached the car. She stepped out into her mother's arms.

"My, how you've grown!" Marie exclaimed. "I can't believe it. Already sixteen years old--and so beautiful. So healthy-looking. Just like the All-American girl!" Then she turned to Lena. "Thank you so much for taking such good care of her." She grabbed Michelle's hand, "Come on in, everyone. We've got so much to talk about."

"That's okay, Marie," Lena started, "Leo and I . . . By the way, you two haven't met." She introduced him to her sister and then continued, "We'll take a skip around town while you get re-acquainted with your daughter. I noticed that Goldman's Best restaurant is still open. Is the food as good as it used to be?"

"I guess so," Marie replied. "Mr. Goldman still owns it, and he still runs the place--at eighty years old!"

"Good. We'll have lunch there. We'll be back in a couple hours."

"Okay. Come on, Michelle, your brothers are waiting to see you again."

Michelle felt as if she had walked into a family hurricane.

When Marie and Michelle got into the house, Jean, now fourteen, and David, who had just turned eleven, were waiting with mixed emotions. Jean hardly remembered his sister, and he wondered how he would feel when they met. David, who did not remember her at all, was not enthusiastic. Her name had been mentioned so much in the past few days that he was satiated and almost wishing that she had not come. So, as mother and daughter entered the living room, they were hit with an awkward moment, but Michelle ignored it and ran to hug the boys that she had coddled when they were babies. Jean returned her hug loosely; David iced up.

Marie signaled Michelle to sit down on the sofa and then she asked the boys to get some Coke for their sister. "I bought it just for you," she whispered, "I remembered that it was your favorite soda."

"Yes," the girl laughed, "And you never wanted me to drink it, except on special occasions! 'It's not good for you', you would say, 'Drink your milk instead'."

"Well, you can have some now," Marie said with a happy gleam in her eyes. "This *is* a special occasion."

"It certainly is," Michelle agreed, as she looked around the room and her hands met in a clap. "Grandmaman's player piano! It's still here!"

"It may be old, but it's still good, though it may be off key," Marie answered. "I remember how you used to plunk *little* tunes on it." She looked squarely at her daughter. "I would never sell it."

Michelle smiled. "I've been taking lessons for a few years now, and I *love* to play. One day I'll be back to get this piano in shape again and I'll play some *big* tunes for you."

"I can't wait to hear you. Ah, here's our snack."

Jean, followed by David, came in with trays of home-made cookies, iced tea for their mother and a large glass of Coke for Michelle.

Marie thanked them, and before they had time to sit down, she sent them away. "Go feed the chickens, or something. I want to spend a few minutes alone with Michelle."

Jean left reluctantly. He was disappointed because he had heard different rumors about his aunt Lena, and he was curious about her and his sister who seemed to come from such a different world.

David, on the other hand, scooted out.

Michelle was eager to hear about all her brothers. Still graven on her mother's mind was Donald, who had died of polio a few years before. As she talked about him, Marie took out her handkerchief with the hand-crocheted border and dotted away her tears. When she got to Henri and Louis, however, her face immediately turned to pride. Both had joined the army and were doing very well. Henri, in fact, was now a staff sergeant, and he was talking of a military career. As for Joe, who was not much older than Michelle, he had joined the Air Force a few months back.

"Why did they all go into the military?" Michelle asked.

"There's not much for them here," Marie's eyes saddened. "It's getting harder to find jobs that pay well. Henri and Louis left school at sixteen and worked in different places, but nothing satisfied them. It wasn't just about the pay, though. They said they wanted to go out and see the world.

With Joe it was different. He got his high school diploma and wanted to be some kind of technician. The Air Force promised to send him to school, so he joined them. He's taking courses in electricity now, and he loves it.

"Well, I certainly wish them well. Now you're left alone with Jean and David. How are they?"

Marie frowned and paused. "I hate to tell you this, but Jean is a lot of trouble."

"Really? He seems quite nice. In fact, they both do. Although I did feel that David was somewhat aloof."

"I brought them up to be polite. But Jean really worries me a lot. He often plays hooky and has gotten into brawls at school. Worse yet, he hangs out with a wild bunch. If he doesn't get away from them, he'll get into real trouble."

This disclosure disquieted Michelle to the core. "Gee, Ma, how are you surviving all this? Your husband in jail, trouble with Jean, not enough money coming in!"

"Day by day," she answered. "My parents loaned me a little money. Hopefully I can make it last till El comes home. As you know, selling eggs won't pay for the mortgage on the house. It does help, though. Every little bit counts."

"What about Jean? What can you do about him?"

"Mr. Masson, the truant officer, has been meeting with him every week. Doing all this on his own time. I thank God every day for that man. Maybe he'll be able to get him away from that gang."

"I sure hope so! What about David?"

"David is fine! He loves school and he helps me a lot around the house. He's a good boy." Just as Marie was saying this, the boys came in and heard it clearly.

It hit Jean like a knife, and he yelled at his mother, "That's because you don't see--or don't want to see what he does! Like yesterday, when you found out that David hit Denis with a rock just because of an argument. You did nothing! If I'd have done that, you would have grounded me for a month! It's not fair!"

He then turned to Michelle. "She didn't believe it. That kid could do something really bad right in front of her, and she wouldn't see it!" He dashed out of the house.

David shrugged his shoulder and left the room.

Michelle felt she had walked into a family hurricane.

"Here he goes again. I just don't understand him," Marie said innocently.

Now it was Michelle's turn not to understand. "But is it true? Did David really hit someone with a rock?"

Marie brushed away the problem with a swish of her hand. "It was just a squabble. You know how kids are."

Michelle was stunned. She had expected to hear about financial problems, but this outburst and her mother's reaction was incredulous and very troubling.

Before Michelle could say anything else, Marie sighed and said, "I'm really doing the best I can."

Michelle looked at her mother, as if for the first time. Her dress seemed to be a size too large, her amber brown eyes were framed by shadows, and subtle blue lines traced narrow veins on her arm. She looked much older than her forty-two years. "I know," she said comfortingly. "This whole situation is just too much for you."

But Marie hardly heard. She was still talking about her eleven-year-old baby. "David's so different from Jean. He's usually at the top of his class. I don't know where he comes from. He's even talking about going to college--as if that could ever happen here." She paused. "I guess he'd have to go into the service, too. I can't bear to think about that."

"Don't be so pessimistic, Ma. Things are changing quickly. If he wants it badly, he'll find a way to go to school without having to go into the military."

"It's easy for you to say that, Michelle. You've got Lena helping you. There's none of her around here. We can't all be Lenas, you know. She's the only one in the family who went away, and she acts as if she's better than all of us. Has all kinds of funny ideas, especially about women. I hope she's not putting things in your head."

Maybe she's the one who's right! almost came out of Michelle's mouth. Upset by her own thinking, she thanked God that she had stopped the words before they hit the air because she certainly didn't want to hurt her mother.

Michelle went white. "That's not true."

As Michelle tried to make sense of everything she had just heard, her own angry feelings began to surface. Like Jean, she too felt that she had been pushed aside. Unconsciously, for years she had nurtured these thoughts and now she was exploding in front of her totally unsuspecting mother. "Why *did* you send me away?" she asked in an accusatory tone. "Why do you like boys better than me? I love you and wanted so much to come help you."

Marie was flabbergasted by her daughter's words and instant turnabout. "What do you mean? Why do you say that?"

Michelle looked around the room. Everything was very clean, but very much worn: a blue and white floral, home-made cover hid the holes in the sofa, the carpet was almost threadbare in some places, the coffee table's blue mirror top had a crack along an edge and most of the furniture was scratched.

"I can see that you've had lots of money problems. So why did you keep on having babies? Is that why you sent me away? You couldn't afford to have me around? Yet, you didn't send any of the *boys* away! Why only me?" She felt like crying, but did not allow the tears to come up. "I love you. Why couldn't you love me? What did I do wrong?"

Marie's countenance jerked in incredulity. "Is *that* what you think? You think that I sent you away because of money problems? You think that I like my boys better than you?"

"Well, what else? I was sure when Leon died. . . how old was he? Three months?. . . I was sure that you would let me come home. But instead you left me with Aunt Lena!"

Marie felt like hugging her "little girl", but she held back. "I guess it's time to talk."

"Ya. I guess it is!" Michelle's lament was filled with frustration.

Marie's small goiter moved, as she swallowed. "My dear child, I didn't realize that you still don't know. I really thought Lena had told you. We've kept this a secret for much too long."

Michelle stiffened. Finally, she would know the truth!

"Your going away had *nothing* to do with money or the boys. Remember the day my mother got very angry with your father when she walked into the chicken coop?"

"Yes, of course, I remember. She was livid. To this day, I have no idea why she was so mad. He was about to give me something nice, and she swishes me off and away without any explanation. Why is everyone so damned secretive?"

"Michelle, she saw what *you did not.*" She sighed, "There's no easy way to say this, child. The fact is your father was about to rape you."

Michelle went white. "That's not true!"

"I'm sorry, honey. So sorry." Marie touched Michelle's hand that had just become limp.

"My own father! I know he beat me a few times. But rape? He would never do that!"

Marie looked straight into Michelle's eyes. "He molested Mrs. Benson's daughter who was only seven." She turned away and kept tapping her fingers on her lap.

Michelle clamped her head with her two hands. "A seven-year-old child? I don't believe this! My father--a rapist? It's horrible to do that to anyone! But surely he wouldn't touch *me!*"

Marie said nothing; her eyes said everything.

Michelle paled and she felt nauseous. After a pause to let her body regain its balance, she said, "I thought he was in jail for beating up someone?"

"He is. The rape was many years ago--about the time you went to Canada. Nothing was ever done about it. Everybody knew, but nobody talked. All they did was tell their kids to stay away from your father. That's all."

Michelle felt as if she had been drawn into the pit of an earthquake. "My own father!" A heavy silence brought her shivers. "What kind of man is he, Ma? How could *you* stand him all these years!"

Suddenly she got dizzy. As the truth made its way into her brain, she felt caught up in a twister that whirled her around and around, and she had no control over where it would drop her. She now realized that everything that she had kept in her heart about her mother and father was the opposite of the truth: Her mother loved her; her father did not. How could he even think of raping her!

Just then, there was a knock on the door and Lena and Leo walked in.

They had stopped at Bellini's Market and came in with a few bags full of groceries for the family. The boys had also just returned and Leo got them to help him put away the produce. Lena, carefully placed her tan cashmere coat on the rack in the front entrance, and as soon as she walked into the living room, she noticed that something was wrong with Michelle. She hastened to go to her.

"I thought you had told her!" Marie's tone was sharp.

Lena stopped as if she had hit a fence. She gulped, looked at her sister, and mumbled, "I couldn't do it." Then she turned to Michelle and said, almost pleadingly, "I tried to tell you, but I just couldn't talk to you about that kind of stuff--not till you were older."

Marie eyed Lena. "You, the liberated lady! I counted on you to tell her. Why didn't you?"

"We all have our Waterloo," Lena said defensively. "Besides, you're her mother. *You* should have told her."

"Lena! I haven't seen my girl since she was six years old! I certainly would never put *that* in a letter!"

Lena calmed down. "I know. I *was* planning to tell her later."

"That's okay, Auntie," Michelle said softly. "Don't worry. This is certainly not everyday conversation material." She got up and hugged her mother for a long time.

Finally, she released her. "I'm so sorry. All along I thought you didn't love me--even after Sr. St. Clara told me that *you did,* and that Papa's surprise was something *bad.* I didn't believe her, although she did put a doubt in my mind about him. I wanted his love so much." As she said this, a memory surfaced, and surprised her very much. "Is that why I went looking for God with JP?" she mumbled.

"Looking for God? And who's JP?" Lena asked.

"A boy I met the summer I stayed at the convent. We had so much fun together." She started to laugh. "One day, we decided to go look for God, the Father. When we saw an old man with white hair and beard, I went to ask him if he was God. Need I say more?" *I was looking for a father?*

They all started to laugh. "Only out of the mouth of Michelle!" Leo jested, as he tipped his hat to her and paused. "Sorry. I keep on forgetting that I have my hat on. It's really *that c*omfortable!" He took it off and placed in on a chalky bust of President Roosevelt that decorated one of the end tables.

"Leo!" Lena's raised eyebrows curved high.

"Okay, okay," he said, as he snatched the hat and went to put in on the hat shelf in the front entrance.

Then Michelle became pensive. Finally she said aloud, "I think it's time for me to let go."

"Let go of what?" Lena asked.

"Of having a loving father." The last words drowned into near silence.

"Well, you do have Leo," Lena proposed. "He may be a little upsetting at times, but he sure loves you."

"Yes, I love Bozo, too," Michelle chuckled. "Hmm. . . Maybe I should consider that."

"Bozo?" Marie asked.

"Private joke!" Michelle answered.

"Well, we'd better get going," Lena announced, as she checked her very gold watch. "It gets dark so early at this time of the year." She went to get her coat and slipped it on while talking. "Well, Marie, I must say, I *am* glad to see you again and to have the opportunity to introduce my husband. What a guy, hey?" She winked at Leo.

"I'm really glad, too," Marie admitted. "Thank you so much for bringing Michelle to see us." Then, for a moment she looked at her daughter and seemed to be absorbing her. Finally, she took her in her arms. "It's been too short a visit. But I'm so happy you came."

"I am too," Michelle smiled, but its brightness was shadowed by the sadness of farewell and by the new, deafening pain in her heart.

As they left and waved goodbye, Michelle shouted, "I'll be back, Ma. I promise."

On the way back home, Michelle cried silently as the truth about her father kept churning in her soul and as she empathized with her mother's hardships. Her whole family situation seemed like an ongoing bad dream. For a moment, she thought of going back home to help her mother, but eventually her father would be out of prison. Now, she felt that she could never, ever face him.

CHAPTER 5

I wish you would have thought of that before!

A few days later, Lena decided it was time to do damage control. By now, it was evident that everyone in the inner circle had succumbed to the gossip about Elphège, and since Gloria was Michelle's best friend, Lena started by calling her mother to try to mend the relationship between those two.

The woman listened courteously, but with little reaction. At the end of the conversation, Lena slammed the handset in its place, spit out a few curse words and went to the kitchen to start dinner. She almost cut off her finger as she sliced through a small tomato. A good thing she had large bandages on hand.

Surprisingly, however, that same evening, Gloria's mother called Lena. She apologized, almost profusely, about her family's reaction. "My husband and I had a long discussion, and we realize that Mr. Bellerose's criminal behavior is not Michelle's fault. In fact, we should have been sympathetic and supportive. I don't know where our head was. When Gloria comes home from her ballet lesson, I'll talk to her."

Lena's first reaction was: *Wish you had thought of that before!* Immediately, however, her thinking pushed that aside and replaced it with: *Leave the past in the past; healing's in the air!* Lena was on a roll again. She decided, though, not to tell Michelle about this conversation until she was sure that Gloria was willing to be friends once more.

The next morning, on the way to school, Michelle kept on telling herself that she must continue to ignore any comments about her father. The minute she saw the building, however, her legs weakened and she stopped to take a deep breath. Then she put on her façade of nonchalance and strolled in.

As she trudged to her locker, she heard "Michelle!" and saw Gloria rushing towards her. *Oh, no! Not just now! Please!* Her body became rigid as she armed herself emotionally against the attack.

"I'm so glad to see you," Gloria cried out, as she hugged her friend in full view of all the students who were meandering in the hallway and who suddenly became spectators. By now almost everyone in school knew about Michelle's father and the breakup of friendships, and they watched this display of amicability with surprise and skepticism.

Michelle pushed her away.

Gloria stepped back. "I just want to tell you how sorry I am that I listened to Jeannette and said I didn't want to be friends anymore."

"You are?" Michelle dropped her locker key. As she stooped to retrieve it, she lost her balance and fell on her knees.

Gloria laughed. "You can say your 'thank you' prayers later on," she commented, as she helped her get up. "I hope this doesn't happen every time I have a surprise for you."

"Thanks," Michelle mumbled, as she hand-brushed the bottom of her skirt. "What made you change your mind?"

"Mom and Dad did. They talked about it a lot and decided it was wrong for us to act like that. I know they're right because I *really* missed you."

"I missed you, too!" Michelle beamed, as *she* now hugged her friend warmly. "But what about Jeannette and the others?"

"I haven't had time to talk to her or anyone else, but just look around," Gloria whispered as she covertly scanned the onlookers. "Guaranteed, the rumor mill is in the making. I'm sure the girls will hear about us before I get a chance to talk to them."

Michelle flushed as she became aware of all the eyes that seemed stalled on her and Gloria.

"Don't worry about them;" Gloria swished her hand in an arc, "I'll take care of the big bad wolf."

Michelle laughed. "I'm okay. I'm just so glad that we're friends again. I hope the others feel the same as you do."

"I hope so, too. I'll do my best to convince them. I'll call you tonight. Gotta go now. Love you." She dashed off.

The bell rang and Michelle ran to her classroom. In her heart a new and sunny day had begun!

The only flaw in that perfect world

The two years that followed brought about meaningful and hopeful changes in Michelle's life. The gossip about her father died slowly but surely, and even Jeannette, whose puffed up mother had incited and maintained the rejection of Michelle, wanted to be friends again.

During that time, Leo became the Chief Financial Officer at the hospital and Lena became a Vice-President at their local credit union. They were climbing the ladder not step by step, but link by link. Lena's lavish parties were like a magnet for the well-do-do, the politicians, and whoever touted their gold jewelry and designer clothes.

Even her parties for the kids made the social scene headlines. They were cool; they were fun; they were hits. And the boys from St. Mark's Academy couldn't wait to be invited, especially since these festivities had a slightly notorious reputation, such as allowing "one on one" close dancing, an activity totally banned by the religious administrators of the two schools the kids attended. This and other such infringements were known to all the parents, however, because Lena wasn't one to hide what she believed and she saw no wrong in this. As for the parents, none of them complained.

Lena felt like a queen, and she kept her king hopping. As he absorbed her energy, Leo went along with her willingly and cheerfully.

Everything was good and Michelle was enjoying her teen-age years to the fullest. She was an honor student in school, won awards for her volleyball feats, was named "student of the year" and was elected president of the senior class. Sparked by her aunt's personal ambition and fired by her almost wearisome encouragement, Michelle aspired to become as successful as her mentor.

The only flaw in that perfect world was Michelle's mother who continued to annoy and worry her daughter by her limited communication and puny information. Whether by greeting card or by phone, when Michelle called her mother, Marie would always insist that everything was okay and that everyone was happy.

Neither Lena nor Michelle believed her. When Michelle gave her aunt the "news" from home, all Lena did was block any further discussion with "I'm glad they're okay".

Their silence, however, would soon be pulverized.

"Don't split the girl in two!"

One month and three weeks before the high school graduation, Grandmaman Cecile telephoned.

Michelle answered.

Lena heard the girl scream.

"My father? No! Please tell me it's not true!"

"I don't want you to hear it from someone else, dear. It *is* true."

"When did that happen?" Michelle's high pitch words resonated throughout the house.

"Yesterday. He had been drinking and, in the middle of the day, he struck a child and kept on going. He was arrested for hit and run resulting in injury and for driving while drunk. He can't afford bail, so he's in jail. Let me speak to Lena."

When Lena heard the news, she went into a hysterical freeze. Although she wanted to explode, everything in her stiffened such as never before and she spoke in a low, calculated tone. "I told her not to marry that lowlife!"

The cold, calm voice unnerved Cecile who was expecting Lena's normal screams and for a few moments, she was speechless.

"Ma! Are you there?" Lena hollered, as she finally let her feelings fly.

"Yes, I am," Cecile barked, "and I'm telling you to leave Marie alone. She has enough problems without your repeating the same thing over and over again. She made a mistake. Leave her alone!"

"You don't get it, do you, Ma. Look what she's doing to our family name!"

"I can't believe you just said that. I sure hope Michelle didn't hear you!" Cecile dove into her. "Your sister and the kids are really suffering because of this, and all you think about is what the neighbors will say. How did I get two such different daughters!"

Lena grunted. "There you go! You always liked her better than me. Marie, the weak, the sickly one! How you sacrificed to help her. Then, what does she do to repay you? She hurts you deeply by marrying that idiot.

Well, that wasn't me! I went to school; I have a career; I was careful to marry someone with class; and

I earned the status that I have now." She stopped to calm her breathing. "Besides all that, I'm taking care of Michelle and I've taught her how to climb and enjoy the wonders that life can bring, if you get educated and work for it. You'll see. One day she'll thank God for living here, and not with her "victim" mother."

Cecile turned into a military sergeant. "Stop talking so loud! I sure hope she's not around to hear you."

"Okay, okay," Lena calmed down reluctantly, I'll. . ."

"Before you go on," Cecile blocked her daughter, "I want you to understand something: Sure, I treated you differently than Marie. Do you know why? It's because you *are* different. You've always been more independent, and I *appreciate* that. I'm very sorry if you took it the wrong way. I did the best I could. I love both of you.

As for as her marriage, yes, it did hurt me. But I got over that *a long time ago*. Now stop demeaning Marie. You'll hurt Michelle. She was so happy to get her mother back. "

"What do you mean?"

"You know what I mean. She's finally convinced that her mother *does* love her. Don't split the girl in two! Do you understand?"

"Yes, yes. Anyhow, thanks for giving us the *good* news," Lena's sarcasm traveled loudly over the phone line.

"Lena!"

"Bye, Ma. I'll talk to you later." She flung the handset into the receiver, turned around and almost bumped into Michelle.

The girl had heard everything. She ran up to her bedroom and the sound of the closing door banged in Lena's head. *I need an aspirin. . . but first a coffee.* She headed for the percolator pot.

"She's manipulating you. Don't you understand?"

For days afterward, Micelle did not want to talk about her father or her mother and the whole house seemed filled with seething volcanic material. Then she received a note from her mother.

Dear Michelle   *April 15, 1956*

I know Grandmaman told you that your father's in prison again. Some people saw him hit the boy. He hurt him bad. Then he drove away. The whole town is angry with him, and even with us. Now some of the kids are harassing the boys. So far, they did not fight back. Every day I tell them to stay out of fights.

To make it worse, the boy is the police chief's grandson! El is having a problem finding a good lawyer.

I feel so bad for that boy and his family.

Don't worry, though. Like I told you before, I do try to find good things in my day.

Love,

Maman

"She's at it again," Lena screeched. "First, all the bad news; then the 'don't worry' bit; and then that nice little ending about 'finding good things' in this damned situation."
"Why does that upset you?"

"She's manipulating you. Don't you understand? Wants you to feel sorry." Her inhale/exhale could have put out a fire, as she walked out of the room.

Michelle read the note again and she still couldn't understand her aunt's reaction. *My mother's just telling me what's been happening and that she's trying to cope with it. What's wrong with that? So what if I feel sorry for her. Is that a sin?*

A few days later, Grandmaman Cecile called to say they had to amputate the boy's leg. There was no doubt about it anymore. El was in real trouble. To make things worse, by now, Jean and David were ready to hit anyone who mentioned their father, and Marie wondered how long she would have the strength to hold down their arms in public, or even at home.

A sense of helplessness went through Michelle's whole body. "What's going to happen now?" she asked her grandmother. "Will Maman have to go to work? She's never worked before. How could she with all the kids she had? And what's going to happen with the boys?"

"We'll help her for a while, honey, at least until Jean's birthday in a few weeks. He can't wait to quit school and get a full-time job. He expects to make a lot of money, of course, but he'll find out it's not that easy. Right now mill jobs, which pay pretty well, are becoming scarce. He may end up in restaurant job or something like that. Time will tell."

"He always said he wanted to have pockets full of money. If he goes to work, do you think he'll give Maman more than board money? Right now, she'll need more than that to survive."

"I'm sure he will. Thanks to Mr. Masson, the Truant Officer. Jean really respects him. Did you know that he helped Jean get out of the gang he had joined?"

"No. When?

"A few months ago. Ever since then, Jean's been behaving better, too. He's much more responsible.

He's even giving your mother the pay from his part-time job right now. She gives him a little pocket money, of course." She paused for a moment. "That kid's been so irresponsible and so much trouble that it's hard to believe that he could change so much. But he has.

For some reason, this seems to upset David, though. Kids! They're sure hard to understand, at times."

Michelle paused, as her thoughts wandered through the good and bad of this information.

"Michelle?" Cecile said loudly.

Her strong voice drew the girl back to the moment. "What if Jean can't earn enough to support the family? What's going to happen?"

"Well, there is a last resort: public assistance. Let's hope it doesn't come to that. Anyhow, I'm so sorry I had to bring you such news, dear. I know it will be hard, but please try not to let it affect your life. Okay?"

She hardly heard Michelle's weak "Okay".

"Good girl. Bye now. I love you, sweetheart."

Love you, too. Bye." When she hung up, Michelle had to lean against the wall. Her heart screamed God! But, at that moment, she neither saw nor heard him

I just can't tell her now!

During the next few weeks, the winds of bad news drowned in the waves of activities and excitement that preceded the coming of graduation day.

Although they were well immersed in the frenzy, however, the "inner circle" still had time for gab sessions, and they soon realized how radically their conversations had changed. Four years of chatter about boys and books had slyly slipped into gab sessions about men and marriage; complaints about high school classes had gradually turned into fears about college lectures; years of schooling were now precursors to future careers; and expectations reaching to the sky were now on the verge of being tested.

Aunt Lena, however, had no such time available. She was too busy planning festivities. She hosted two parties to perfection: one just for girls where they could be free to "girl talk" all night long; the other, mixed, where they could dance and flirt, and maybe steal a few kisses behind the bushes that circled their new, lighted patio.

Leo, who had been appointed "Party Chaperone par Excellence", watched like a hawk, but never saw anything unless it was going "too far". In those few instances, he not only interrupted the behavior but gave the unsuspecting kids his own brand of sermon: short and frank enough to make them blush. For that alone, they would never repeat such misbehavior, at least not when Leo was around.

In the meantime, Lena and Michelle spent days making plans for a summer vacation and for the beginning of college in September. Michelle had been accepted in the Education program at Boston College, a very notable institution in Massachusetts. Since the late 1920's they had been gradually accepting women in their degree programs, a fact that impressed Lena greatly. Michelle could have gone to a reputable women's college, but they both felt that a coed education would be a different type of challenge, and one that Michelle was eager to take on.

Finally graduation day arrived and Michelle had the honor of being the salutatorian. Her short speech drew as much *applause* as that of the valedictorian and Leo and Lena would not have been prouder had she been their own daughter.

"Too bad her mother can't be here to see this," Leo whispered to his wife.

"I guess so," was all that Lena answered.

The graduation party lasted into the early morning hours, and the next day, no one got up till almost noontime. Michelle was the first to rise and she tiptoed down to the pantry. After making coffee, she poured herself a mug-full, settled near a large window in the kitchen and stared into the distance. The high noon sun was shining gloriously outside; but in the room everything was in shadow. *Just as in my head,* she concluded, as she grew aware that the dimness around her reflected the uncertainties in her mind--troublesome thoughts that had kept her awake most of the night. *I can't go on like this,* she ruminated, *I have to find a solution.*

An hour later, she was still sitting at the window when she heard Lena padding softly down the stairs.

Michelle started to sweat and kept on looking outside.

"So, how's the new graduate?" Lena said cheerily.

"Fine." She did not turn to greet her aunt.

"Oh? Well, you don't look too fine to me. The party was too much last night, hey?" She hurried to the pantry.

"No. It was okay."

"Okay? I haven't seen you that upbeat in months. Every time I spied on you, you seemed to be having lots of fun. Especially with Jim. Girl, he sure has his eyes on you." She stretched to grab an oversized mug on the top shelf of the cupboard.

"I did have fun, Auntie," she mumbled. *I have to tell Lena, but not now. I can't do it now.* She gulped the rest of her coffee and continued staring out the window.

"Well, what is it, then? The day-after-Christmas blues?" Lena laughed. "That's a no-no in June!" She brought her maxi mug to the coffee maker and filled three-quarters of it with coffee and the rest with cream. Then she took a quick sip and opened another cupboard door. "Leo will be down in a minute. . . ah, here's the pancake mix." Setting it on the counter, she then went to Michelle. "I should be starting the pancakes, but I can see something's wrong here. What's going on?

Just then Leo walked in. "Good morning, girls! A new day begins!" His outrageous grin and buffoonish attitude brought an actual smile from Michelle.

"We're just having a little chit chat," Lena said, "Start the pancakes. We'll be famished in a few minutes."

"Pancakes comin' up, for the 'famished femmes' " he said, as he swung open the refrigerator door and took out eggs and milk.

I hope I marry someone like him," Michelle said sincerely, as she watched him take his position as the day's breakfast chef.

"Never mind him, Michelle. What is it? What's going on?" Lena was becoming very uneasy.

I just can't tell her now. Michelle smiled weakly. "It's not urgent. I'll tell you later. Right now I just want those pancakes."

"Not true. I know you better than that. What's on your mind? I want to know *now.*"

Michelle gulped. "Okay. Here it is. I don't want to travel this summer. I want to go home to help my mother."

Lena's coffee spilled on her new satin robe and Leo dropped the last egg on the floor.

Michelle waited for Lena's scream. When it came a moment later, it actually made waves in her coffee.

"You can't do that! I won't let you!" her aunt commanded, as she tried futilely to wash away the stain on her robe.

"Dd…ddid you ever try to pick up broken eggs on the floor?" Leo stuttered for the first time since he was nine.

"Damn the eggs!" Lena cried out to him. "Did you hear what she just said?"

"Why the hell do you think I dropped the egg?" he said, as he swiftly swooped up the yellow slush with a paper towel, flung it into the trash and came over to her. "Calm down, Lena. It's not the end of the world!" Then he turned to Michelle, "Why do you want to do that?"

"I want to be with my mother. I want to go help her."

"I knew the manipulation would work! Now the whole summer will go to waste! You can't do that! Why do you want to mess up all our plans?"

Helping my mother is not a waste of time," Michelle insisted with her eyes as well as with her words.

"Well, I didn't mean it that way. It's just that. . ."

Leo interrupted. "You're a very compassionate girl," he told Michelle, "but you haven't been there for over two years and your mother's been surviving. Going there at this time may be more of a problem than a help. She has enough problems already."

"So, you do admit that she has problems!" the girl answered.

"Of course. Doesn't everyone?"

"Well, we certainly don't have *that kind* of problem! She loved me enough to send me away so that my father would not hurt me. Now, I love her enough to go help her." She sprang up, went to the pantry and almost cracked her coffee mug as it hit the counter.

Lena stopped rubbing her coffee stain and followed Michelle. "After that last letter, I figured that sooner or later it would come to something like this. You have no idea what you're getting into! I just can't let you do that."

"I'm sorry, Auntie, but I'm eighteen now and no one can stop me." Her eyes spoke with a boldness that surprised Lena. She always nurtured confidence in Michelle, but she surely never expected it to boomerang to her.

The couple eyed one another. "We can't stop her," Leo shrugged. "More importantly, we should not. It's her life, her decision."

Lena whirled and dashed off. "Forget the pancakes. I'm not hungry." Then she stopped and stared at Michelle. "Just remember that you'll have to live with the consequences of this decision forever! Whatever that will be."

Michelle walked over to her aunt. "Thank you. I'll be okay. Everything will be okay. I know it. I'll be back in time to get my college wardrobe. And then it'll be 'Boston, here I come!'"

Lena knew she wouldn't win. Even Leo wasn't on her side. Slowly her flushed face paled to normal and she looked like a soldier who had just surrendered. "I'll miss you so much. We were supposed to do so many things together." Then she continued very curtly. "Do what you have to do. When do you want to go?"

"As soon as possible," Michelle answered excitedly. "I'm going to call Gloria. I'll miss her, but I can't wait to go home. I'm not hungry anymore." She ran out.

Lena gave Leo a disapproving nod. "I'm not very hungry anymore."

Leo picked up the ingredients for the batter. "I guess we'll wait for the pancakes. I'll make a few toasts." He put away the eggs and milk and took out the bread.

Lena sat at the table and waited. She didn't even have the energy to go fill her cup.

CHAPTER 6

"Now don't go tell that to Lena!"

Three days later Michelle was back in Mapleview. Leo had driven her up, but Lena had stayed behind. However, she had sent several bags filled with a large beef chuck, potatoes, turnips, onions, carrots, apples, and oranges, to be delivered by Leo. Marie was pleasantly surprised by this gift, but she was sorry that her sister had not come. When Leo finished unloading the bags, Marie offered him some homemade pie. At first he was hesitant, but then he decided to accept.

"Just a small piece, please. Gotta watch my weight, you know," he said, as he tapped his belly and took a seat at the table. A few minutes later, he had before him a mountain of golden crust over a thick layer of savory pieces of apples. His very first bite ended up in a loud exclamation, "This is dee. . .licious!"

Michelle and Marie chuckled and chatted as they ate their small pieces and watched Leo's pie disappear. When he finished, Marie offered him a second helping.

"Please!" He handed her his plate.

"From the plate to the pounds!" Michelle warned him mischievously.

"Who cares?" he answered instantly. "I need one for the road!" He plunged his fork into the luscious crispy crust.

"This is the best pie I ever tasted," he complimented Marie, as he scooped up the remnants on the dish and then wiped his mouth with a small, cloth napkin. "Now don't go tell that to Lena," he warned Michelle. "This has to be our private secret."

Michelle laughed. "I won't say a word--ever!"

"Good. Now I'd best be going." Then he turned to Marie, "Your daughter's a real sweetheart."

Marie glanced at Michelle. "I know," she responded.

I wish this was a bad movie, but it isn't.

About an hour later, David came home with his two friends. Michelle was going to hug him, but, she could feel him stiffen and she simply greeted him warmly. He returned her "hello" and the trio ran upstairs to go play games.

Around suppertime, Jean returned from his new job. Michelle approached to give him a big hug, but he remained rigid, said a polite "Nice that you could come," and disappeared into his room.

Michelle felt as if she had just been locked out. She shrugged and returned to help her mother who was checking on the roast and potatoes that were sending salivating smells throughout the house. "Is there something wrong with Jean?"

"No. . . I don't think so. Why?" She picked at the roast with a long fork. "It's almost ready."

"He just didn't seem the same." Michelle opened one of the cupboard doors. "Where are the plates?"

"On the other side," Marie answered, as she took the bread out of the oven. "He must have had a bad day at work. It happens sometimes."

"Oh. . . Well, that must be it." Michelle agreed, but inside she remained dumbfounded.

At suppertime the conversation was even more baffling. David let his feelings fly. He raved about the roast and devoured it with such gusto that Michelle realized this was not common fare for them. Jean, on the other hand, was quiet and unnaturally polite, although his eyes and utensils couldn't stay off the food. As soon as he finished eating, he excused himself, said "goodnight" and went to sit outside on the porch.

When David got through, he helped clear the table, and then went to join his brother.

That night Michelle lay in bed reflecting on her life and everything that had happened in just a few hours. *What a difference a day makes*, she thought, as her eyes wandered around the room. In Oakton her white French Provincial bed was covered with a light blue satin quilt, a pillow stuffed in a satin sham, and a bed ruffle trimmed with French lace. The rest of the spacious room was furnished with matching furniture: a dresser, wardrobe, desk, free-standing mirror and a bedside table that showed off an antique lamp with genuine crystals dangling like icicles around the lower edge of its silk shade.

This was about half the size of her bedroom in New Hampshire, and it was sparsely furnished with maple furniture: a twin bed, a small night table, a huge four-drawer bureau, and a rocking chair. A flowery, hand-painted ceramic lamp with a cardboard-like shade provided the only light in the room.

The quilt on this bed was far from being satin, but she loved it. Gently and lovingly she brushed it with her hand, feeling the tiny stitches around the varied and dissimilar pieces of fabric that made up the blanket. How well she remembered watching her mother diligently building it up by sewing strips of cloth that neighbors had given her. *At the time she already had five children,* Michelle thought, *and she still took the time to make this quilt.* Slowly, she brought it up to her lips and kissed it. How warm and comforting it felt.

Then her brothers' voices in the hallway sneaked in and reminded her of Jean's unusual behavior since she arrived. He had seemed so glad to see her the first time she visited. Why was he so aloof now? Confused, but very tired, she went to sleep.

The next evening, after supper, everyone was in the living room listening to the radio. Jean was doodling on a sheet of scrap paper, Marie was teaching Michelle how to knit, and David was doing a crossword puzzle.

Suddenly Jean jumped up. "Listen! They're talking about him."

"About who?" David asked.

"About our father. Weren't you listening?"

Marie and Michelle dropped their knitting.

"The sentencing is next week. It's next week, Ma. Next week!" Jean screamed. "How come we didn't know?"

Marie sat down. "Looks like the radio folks got the information before we did."

Michelle eased in next to her mother on the sofa and put her arms around her.

"Well, he'll finally get what he deserves," Jean said, as his jagged, heavy scribbling almost cut through the paper.

"Hey, he's your father. Don't talk like that," Marie replied sharply.

"I don't care! He's never been a father to me, anyhow!"

"Well, *I* miss him," David said mournfully.

"Ya. Sure!" Jean exploded. "He brought you fishing all the time. Me? Never! I was only good to clean the chicken coop and walk around their crud to feed them-- and things like that. Anyhow, I don't wish him bad things; I just want him to get what he deserves. Gee! Can't you see! He maimed a child!" He stuck his pencil into the hole of a small, hand-held sharpener.

"He didn't bring you because you don't like fishing!" David argued.

"I could have gone, just to hang around," Jean replied. "I didn't *have* to fish. I wouldn't have bothered anybody."

David looked straight at his brother. "That would never have worked with Papa. You know that."

"Ya. I sure do." This time his newly-sharpened pencil tip tore the paper.

"Anyhow, he didn't mean to hurt anyone!" David said defensively. "He was drunk."

"Well, he didn't have to get drunk, did he?" Jean eyed his brother. "How many times did we tell him not to get drunk. He never listened, did he? And how do you think that boy's parents feel, hey?" He stopped to catch his breath. "And by the way, I saw him give *you* some whiskey that day. Were you drunk, too?"

"Stop that!" Marie commanded. "It's your father who did wrong. Don't bring David into this."

Jean went straight to Michelle. "There you are! See! This kid is never wrong." His eyes then darted to his mother. "Now that you know, why don't you tell him he's not supposed to drink booz? If it were me, you'd be on my back for sure."

Michelle watched in dismay. *Nothing has changed*, she thought. *It's a repeat of two years ago. I wish this was just a bad movie, but it isn't!*

Almost growling, Jean turned to Michelle again and pointed at David. "And did you know that he's not too happy that you're here? Because now he thinks Maman likes you better than him." He paused. "Good. I'm glad I said that. Now he knows how it feels to be pushed aside."

Michelle and Marie gasped.

"Is that true?" Marie asked David.

The boy did not answer.

"David! Is that true?" For the first time, Michelle saw Marie's eyes flare.

"Maybe. But you know what? I just changed my mind. Now I'm glad she's here because *he* won't be able to boss me anymore."

"Ha ha!" Jean snorted as he pointed at Michelle. "Now *she'll* do it!"

"Oh God. I feel so dizzy." Marie slid into the back cushion of the sofa.

The boys dashed off in opposite directions and Michelle sat still as she absorbed what she had just seen and heard. Her body quivered as she realized that it was not only her mother who needed help; it was everyone living in that house!

Her very first reaction was to call her aunt and pack her bags. But in the heavy quiet of the "after storm", her mother's soft weeping reached her, and Michelle moved over to cuddle her.

Maybe she'll always be helpless.

The next day, when everyone had calmed down, things returned to their abnormal normal: from one to ten, communication was at level 1 and tension was at 9. Anyone coming in would surely have assumed that it was only because of the impending trial, but they would have been wrong.

In mid-morning, still troubled by the whole situation, Michelle found refuge on the porch. It was already very hot, and in the shadow of their comforting oak tree, she rocked in the aged wicker chair and thought about Leo's words. *Maybe he's right. Now I'm the problem? I really, really shouldn't be here.*

Then she heard her mother's footsteps, and instantly she thought of Marie's total lack of command in yesterday's emotional storm. *Aunt Lena's right,* she ruminated. *Maman made wrong choices and now she can't deal with them. They're her problems, not mine.*

Maybe she'll always be helpless. I can't do anything about that. I should go back to Oakton.

At that very moment, Marie walked up to Michelle with an armful of freshly-picked flowers from her garden. "I cut these just for you. They'll look so beautiful in your bedroom." She spread them on the small table that matched the chair and hurried away to get a vase.

"Thanks, Ma, they're gorgeous." Michelle's words followed Marie, "You're a great gardener."

"It's my little heaven," Marie said animatedly, as she returned with a lovely blue glass vase. "When I'm working in the garden, I'm at peace with myself and with the world. And when I see everything in bloom, I feel so happy. How I love my garden."

Michelle had seldom seen her mother so impassioned, and it impressed her deeply. *Somewhere in her*, she thought, *there is a place--and a desire--for happiness; she's not hopelessly helpless.*

"There we are," Marie was saying, "What do you think?" She raised the vase and proudly presented her tasteful floral arrangement to her daughter.

Michelle got up to accept the gift. "It's beautiful! You did a wonderful job, Ma. I'll bring it upstairs right now." She strolled into the house, holding the vase as if it were sacred.

Marie was as pleased as a child.

As she walked up to her bedroom, Michelle kept sniffing the flowers and thinking about her mother. By the time she placed the vase on her night table, she had arrived at a definite and final decision. She *was* staying. Her mother's moment of passion had convinced her. *Maybe she can be helped; maybe I can help. I will surely try.*

The rest of the week went by quickly. Everyone kept very busy: David was out with his friends from morning till suppertime; Jean's hours at work had increased to full time, and since he also took all the

72

overtime they offered, he was seldom home; and Marie managed her days by making sure the house was scrupulously spotless. She couldn't sit down without seeing specks of dust that had to be swished away and, at night, though exhausted, she had to take a sleeping pill.

Michelle had her old job back, taking care of the chickens and their housing. The first time she went into the yard and started spraying the feed, unexpected emotions surfaced like storm waves hitting the beach. As she swished her hand back and forth, scattering grains in all directions, she could almost hear her father calling: "You'll really like it. Come on."

I had such a distorted image of him--and of my mother, she thought, as an uneasy shiver traveled round and round her whole body. *All caused by that one ugly incident. And then the years of emotional pain that followed! What confusion and harm distorted images can bring!*

All of a sudden, Marie let out a subdued, painful cry.

Marie and the boys had attended Elphège's trial, but on the day of sentencing, she felt sick, and did not want to go. However, bothered by David's insistence that she *should* go, she finally gave in. Jean, however, was in no mood to ask for a day off for that.

At 6:30 a.m. Michelle, Marie and David quietly embarked on their journey to the courthouse in Montpelier. The two-hour drive seemed endless. A few nervous remarks from one or the other only added to the heaviness in their hearts.

Upon arrival at the site, they left the car in a nearby parking lot and walked to the courthouse which held within its confines the balance of their life. Although they were not on trial, each of them would feel the pain and the weight of the Scale of Justice. They held hands and slowly went up the stairs.

As they entered the court room and sat down on the benches, Michelle felt a lump in her throat. *I just can't believe this is happening. God, I can't believe it! But it is.*

Ten minutes later, the side door opened and the lawyers came in. They were soon followed by a guard leading a handcuffed Elphège to his place.

Michelle had not seen her father in ten years, and she was glad she was sitting down. His black hair was now streaked with gray and he looked much older than she expected. He walked in head high, cast a glance toward them and swiftly turned away, as if he had not recognized anyone.

All of a sudden, Marie let out a subdued, painful cry, hurled her palm toward her heart and grabbed Michelle's hand. "Take me out of here!"

"Stay here," Michelle said to David, as she jumped up, put her arms around her mother, and they quickly left the room.

Once in the hallway, Marie was in such pain that she could hardly move. Michelle led her to the bench just outside the courtroom and shouted to the security guard standing in the lobby. "Please, call for an ambulance. My mother's sick."

Within minutes, the guard made the phone call and returned to check on the sick woman. He stayed with Marie while Michelle ran back into the courtroom to tell David what was happening.

When she asked if he wanted to stay or go to the hospital, he was so anxious about the outcome of the sentencing that she made the decision for him. "Stay. I'll come back to get you." Then she rushed to her mother's side, just as the ambulance team arrived.

Two hours later, Michelle had picked up David and they were finally allowed to see their mother who had experienced an angina attack.

David had never been in a hospital and his face turned white when he saw his mother, pale and immobile, hooked to tubes and meters.

"I'm so sorry," Marie said weakly and looked soulfully at Michelle.

"About what?" Michelle asked in surprise.

"All this trouble that I'm causing you."

"How can you even think like that, Ma? It's not your fault. Besides, I'm glad to be here to help you."

"That's what I mean, Michelle. You came to visit, and here you are caught in my problems. I never wanted that to happen."

"I came here to see all of you and to help in anyway that I can. Right now I'm darned glad to be here. I'd be much more worried if I were far away." She went to kiss her mother. "Please, Ma. stop that kind of thinking. You'll never get better if you're always worried."

David was getting white. He plopped on a bedside chair, his eyes frozen on his mother.

Michelle sat on the edge of the bed. "Listen, Ma, I can't make you get well. *You* have to do that. But I can help you. In fact, we'll all help you, won't we, David?"

He jumped up and took his mother's hand. "I'm so sorry, Maman. I shouldn't have argued with you this morning. I didn't know you were so sick. This is all my fault."

"No, no! Don't think like that!" Marie's voice was weak but pleading. "This would have happened sooner or later. Honest."

Michelle put her hand on his shoulder. "Come on, David. It's *not* your fault. Did you tie a noose around her neck and drag her to court?"

A wry smile flashed on his face, but his color did not change.

Marie sighed heavily. "Thank you. You're wonderful kids." Then she dared to ask what had been on her mind for hours. "David, what happened at the trial?"

"Six years in prison and a $500 fine." David felt his throat tighten and the anxiety that had been increasing in his heart day by day steamed out in almost uncontrollable tears.

Michelle put her arms around him and, for a moment, he let his head fall on her shoulder. When he let go, Michelle said to her mother, "I guess it's useless to say 'don't worry', but things *will* work out, Ma. I promise."

"Just wait for emotions to calm down. . ."

A few days later, Marie was discharged from the hospital, and Michelle made super efforts to create a positive environment in the home. But it all seemed futile. The only refuge was the piano. It had been tuned and Michelle spent some time every day playing for her mother, who adored classical music and watched with pride as her daughter's fingers rippled rapidly over the keys. For both, It was the only escape from the disquieting pall that covered the hearts of everyone, each for different reasons: Marie, because her husband and provider was gone; David, because his father was gone; Jean, because everyone was in the pits, and because Michelle was here; Michelle because she ached for everyone.

Jean was still upset with his father, but he did not feel a sense of loss. David, on the other hand, felt a vacancy that no one could understand--except Michelle. In a way, the same thing had happened to her, albeit for very different reasons. No matter how much she tried, she still could not completely eradicate the sense of "loss of a father" that seemed engraved in her emotions.

As the days passed, however, these feelings got repressed as she focused on her brothers and tried to understand them better. Little by little she began to see things that, heretofore, had gone unnoticed.

Jean, she soon found out, was deep down, a very good- hearted person. In fact, for all the trouble he had given his mother in the past, now he genuinely wanted to help her. After a while, she concluded that his new position in the family--taking his father's place--gave him a sense of worth and increased his self-esteem. He no longer had to resort to outlandish behavior to be "somebody", and he didn't have a competitor: his father. Now, however, she understood why he didn't like to have *her* around, and she determined to do everything in her power to assure him that she had no intention to replace him. He was still in charge.

David, though, was still fearful that his sister was replacing him in his mother's esteem. Michelle understood this but didn't know how to handle the situation, except to ignore his underhanded comments and continue to encourage him and his endeavors in every way she could imagine.

One day, however, he irritated her so much that she felt like whacking him. Then she remembered Aunt Lena's advice that it's usually better to be truthful about one's feelings than to hide them. "Wait for emotions to calm down, then be real honest about your feelings," Lena said. "But remember, you're not on a one-way street, so give the other person the opportunity to speak his piece, too. Comprends-tu? That's how you'll find a way to resolve the problem."

So, Michelle decided to have a long talk with David--and with her mother--and do it quickly. It was already mid July, and she only had a few more weeks left before returning to Oakton.

But her journey was about to take another turn.

By the end of July, Michelle felt that she was accomplishing nothing, and a depression was in the process of overwhelming her.

Marie's health was not improving as quickly as the girl had anticipated, the boys were still involved in tensions, and Jean's salary was not sufficient to pay for food, house bills, and now medicine. David tried to help by weaving his way into an "under the table" dishwasher job, but what he earned just about paid for a bottle of aspirin. And Michelle continued to dip into her personal savings account to pay for her board as well as to help with the doctors and medicine.

However, the reason for the darkness that rumbled in her soul had nothing to do with those things. Her problem was with her father, or rather, with her unresolved anger with him. The more she thought of him, the angrier she got; the angrier she got, the more depressed she felt.

I can't continue like this, she finally decided. *I have to do something to get this out of my brain. I have to face him and tell him how I feel.*

Two days later, on Saturday, she drove to the state prison. Although the institution was just two hours away from Mapleview, the ride seemed endless. By the time she arrived at the visitor's lot, she considered making a U-turn and heading back home, but she changed her mind as she spotted a parking space. It was very narrow and she let out a few choice words as she wiggled her car in-between the two trucks that blocked her view on both sides.

Once settled in, she languored in the car for ten minutes, going back and forth with the option of leaving. Finally, she got out and struggled up the cement stairs.

As she followed the guard to the visitors' section, her thumping heart and her tic-tacking high heels competed for attention in the long, echoing corridor. *Why am I doing this? Maybe I should go back. No. I have to do it!*

Then the guard opened the thick door that led into a small room where a few straight chairs were settled in front of a counter that ran the length of one wall and separated the visitors' section from the prisoners' cubicles. It was lined from top to ceiling with prison bars through which the visitors and inmates could communicate.

The muddy green walls and the cool, concrete floor only aggravated her mood as she picked the chair at the first station and sat down, her crossed leg kicking back and forth and her hands and feet getting clammy.

Finally, the door to the cubicle opened and Elphège walked in. Now that he was so close to her, Michelle noticed how the lines on his face gave him a severe look and how his narrow eyes, peeking through slits made her feel uneasy. This is not how she remembered her father and she wondered how this could be. Had he changed that much? Or had *she* idealized him that much?

As soon as he sat across her, he extended his hand and said, "Michelle, my little Michelle."

She did not return his gesture. "How are you?"

"Could be better. They don't serve booz here." he quipped.

Michelle's face was enough to tell him that she was not impressed with this unconscionable attempt at wit.

He scratched his forehead. "Well, you sure have grown, little girl. Turned out to be real pretty. How's the big boss, Lena?"

"She's fine. She's been very good to me," Michelle informed him curtly.

"I suppose so."

Long pause.

"Don't you want to know how Maman and the kids are doing?"

He started to turn his head from left to right. "Sorry, I do this a few times every hour. Muscle problem. Sure. How are they?"

Michelle was ready to get up and scream. "You don't even look concerned. Don't you think of anyone but yourself?"

He stopped his neck rolling and looked at her. "Of course, I do. So, tell me. How *are* they?"

"Maman's not well, but the boys are fine." Immediately she added, "They *will* survive."

"I doubt it. Marie needs me too much. Too bad they had to stick me in here for so long, hey?"

His words hit Michelle like stones. "Have you no heart? Is that all that you care about: that Maman be dependent on you? Is that why you married her? Didn't you love her?"

"Hey! Sure I did. But growing up and having a family is not just about love. Sometimes it's there, and sometimes it ain't. I did what I had to do, and so did your mother. Now she's alone. Nothin' I can do about it. They should have thought of that before giving me six years. Anyhow, it ain't my fault if she's like that, so don't come accusing me of things."

Michelle put her two hands on her stomach. "I feel nauseous." She waited as the bile finally quieted.

"Why are you here sounding like you do?" Elphège snapped and then seemed to be thinking. "Is it because you were sent to Canada? I had nothin' to do with that. In fact, I couldn't believe it when they told me my little girl was gone. I was mad like hell."

Michelle got up and stared at him. "Is that so? Then why didn't you write to me? Maman did!"

"Come on, Michelle. You know I don't write. I sure did miss you, though."

"Right! And, by the way, what about that nice present that you were going to give me in the chicken coop? Why didn't you send it to me? A nice present from my loving father. That would have been really nice to get when I was so far away from home!"

He put his elbow on the counter, scratched his head and stared at the counter. "I don't know what you're talking about."

"Well, let me tell you why I came here today." She paused and eyed him like an arrow ready to be shot. "That day, long ago. . . in the chicken coop. I know what you were going to do. How could you! How could you even think of it!"

"Hey, I don't know what they told you. Cecile's always exaggerating about things. You know she don't like me. What did she say I was gonna do?"

"You know very well that you were planning to rape me! How could you even think of it! Thank God Grandmaman came in and saw what was going on!" By now Michelle's face was almost steaming.

His hand swished in a quick curve. "Hey, don't get so hopped up. It ain't worth having a heart attack."

Michelle froze her scream. Instead, controlled, deliberate words left her mouth. "Do you really believe what you just said?"

His eyes turned away from Michelle and his lips pursed back and forth. He gave no response.

"All those years I had no idea what had really happened, so I always kept hoping that you loved me, even though they told me you did not." She stopped and replayed Elphège's recent words in her head. "You don't even have regrets about it! Where in the world do you come from?"

He winced. "Hey, what do you want me to do. What's done is done. Besides, I never did touch you, did I?"

"Because you were stopped! How dare you! I can't believe this!" She started pacing, then took a very deep breath and returned to him. "Nothing bothers you? What about that boy who lost his leg because of you? You don't even seem to be concerned about that!"

"Hey, I was drunk. I wouldn't have done that sober."

"That's not an excuse to be cold and uncaring." She stopped, let out a shivering exhale and paused. "You know, I'm already beginning to feel better. I thought I hated you, but I don't. I *pity* you and truly hope and pray that sooner or later something will touch that heart of steel." She turned and walked away.

He watched her speed to the door. Then, just as she grabbed the handle, he called, "Wait! Come back. I have something to tell you."

Michelle hesitated. Then she loosened her grip. "What is it?"

"I have a message for you." He signaled her to approach.

"What is it?" she asked with guarded curiosity and walked back to him.

He leaned towards her. "There's a prisoner here who knows you."

"A prisoner?"

"Yep, I've been working with him. Remembers you from a long time ago. One guess."

"I have absolutely no idea who you're talking about."

"How about a JP?

"JP? Jean Paul Larivière?" Michelle's mouth stayed open.

"That's it! We peeled potatoes together a few days ago, and he told me that he remembers you from Canada."

Michelle's fingers tapped her mouth. "Oh God."

"He said to say 'hello' to you. After your little outburst a while ago, I wasn't going to tell you, but hey, why not? Besides it just shows that your friends are no better than me."

Michelle folded onto the chair. She didn't really want to know, but finally her curiosity won. "What's he here for?"

Elphège grinned. "Robbery and aggravated assault."

Michelle's face blanched. "Robbery?"

"Yep. The whole nine yards: Robbery and assault-- aggravated!" he emphasized, and continued nonchalantly, "He says he'd really like to talk to you."

"Why?"

"How should I know! Maybe he's got his eye on you. How'd you meet him, anyhow?"

"It doesn't matter. My goodness, I was only seven! I have to go." She jumped up and hurried away.

Elphège shrugged his shoulders and grinned as he watched her leave; but as the door closed, his smile dissipated, and he walked slowly back to his cell.

It's almost time to leave, and nothing is resolved here.

Outside the prison, Michelle stopped, closed her eyes and breathed in gallons of fresh air before returning to her car. As she did so, memories floated in and out of her consciousness and her feelings about her father were pushed aside by remembrances of JP. *We had so much fun together. I really liked him. . . I can't believe this. . . Something sure changed him. . . It can happen to anyone, I guess.*

By the time she opened her car door, her father was on top of the haunting pile again. "Telling him off" had made her feel better for a few minutes, but now she realized that it had not brought peace or closure. Impatiently, she worked her way out of the parking slit, sped around the rows of driverless cars and practically hit a fence post as she made a right turn at the exit. *I should never have come here,* she thought, as she rolled into the highway traffic.

As she whizzed along the road, JP fought with El for first place in her thoughts: her feelings about her father kept being interrupted by his surprising disclosure of JP's incarceration and message. "Says he'd like to see you." spun in her head like a broken record and as she neared home she realized that it would not stop bothering her unless she found out what he wanted.

When she got home, the first thing she did was go to her calendar. Under July 24, she wrote, "Visit JP".

Then she saw a note from her mother: "Lena called. She wants you to call her."

Oh, Oh! Reluctantly, she went to the phone and dialed. "Hi, Auntie."

"How are you?" Lena chirped happily.

"Okay," the girl answered dryly. Then, bringing up her tone a level or two, "How's everything down there?"

The perceptive aunt, however, zeroed in on the "Okay". "Hey, do I sense a little down mood?"

"No. Everything's fine."

But Lena wasn't convinced. "What's going on? Is your mother still sick?" She began to sound jittery.

Michelle's response was slow and cautious. "Yes. . . but she's getting better every day. . . And Jean has a full-time job now. We're all okay."

"Well, I sure hope so. For a moment, you scared me. Anyhow, it's almost time for you to come back. We can come get you next Saturday, the 24th. That'll give you time to get your college wardrobe. I can't wait. It'll be so much fun going shopping with you again. . . Michelle. . . Are you there, Michelle?"

Michelle kept staring at "Visit JP" on her calendar. "Yes. I'm here. Let me think about it. I'll call you in a few days."

"Why can't you answer now?"

Silence. . . "Michelle! Why am I getting a bad feeling about this conversation? What's wrong?"

"Nothing. I just have to settle a few things here before I go. Just a moment, I'll check my calendar." The handset went down with her arm and she totally ignored the calendar before her. She just wanted time to think.

"Michelle! Are you there?" Lena's voice bellowed.

The handset jumped back to Michelle's ear. "Ah, here it is. I should be ready by the next day, the 25th. I'll call you."

"Okay. But don't wait too long. We have to go visit the college in a few weeks. And while we're there, we can go shopping in Boston."

"Okay. I'll call you soon. Love you." She closed the phone and dropped on the first available chair. *It's almost time to leave and nothing is resolved here. Nothing.*

Then she heard her mother. "Is that you, Michelle?"

"Yes."

"Did you call Lena? She was very eager to talk to you."

Michelle's steps were slow and heavy, as she went into the kitchen. "I did, Ma. No problem. We're all set." She gave her mother a kiss.

"What did she want?"

"For one thing, she can't wait to go shopping for my college wardrobe."

Marie stopped chopping the onions. "Will you be leaving soon?"

"Yes, but not right away. I have a few things to do before I go. Now what can I do to help you?"

"For starters, you might go get some basil in the garden."

"Great! I can taste it already. I'll be right back." When she got outside, she paused at the garden. For some reason, today it seemed more captivating than ever, and she marveled at how her mother had managed to blend a mixture of flowers and herbs into such a masterpiece. *I'll miss this. How I will miss it!*

"If you don't believe me, I'll understand."

The next Saturday, Michelle was at the prison again. At 2 p.m. sharp, she walked into the room where she had met her father the week before, sat down on the hard, wood chair and waited. She could feel her heart beating fast, as she anticipated meeting her childhood friend. *I wonder what he looks like. Why does he want to see me?*

Then her thoughts were diverted as another woman came in with a teenage boy. She sent a quick smile to Michelle, and the two went to the station at the opposite end of the room. Sullenly, she thought of her father. *He didn't even ask to see Maman or the boys. I'll never understand it. No matter. If David wants to come, I'll bring him to visit before I leave. Maybe Maman will want to come, too.*

A few minutes later, JP appeared. At nineteen years old, he was lean and at least six feet tall. The small lock of dark hair that had perpetually hung on his forehead when they played in the convent yard was still swinging with his movements, and his grayish blue eyes matched, sad to say, the gray prison outfit that seemed too large for him. They had a spark, however, that no prison wall or prison garb could ever dull.

After a moment's hesitation, he sprinted towards his place and quickly took a chair. Totally forgetting his situation, he looked straight at her. "I can't believe it's really you! Maybe you won't believe me, but I often wondered what had happened to you. This is such an unexpected surprise." Then as the reality of the moment came back to him, his voice dipped into an apology. "How awful to have to meet in a place like this! Thank you so much for coming."

"I must admit I was shocked when my father told me about you. Even more, when he said you wanted to see me. How did you know that he's my father?"

"Well, I never forgot you--or your family name. Bellerose fits you so well." His smile stretched from cheek-to-cheek and his narrowed eyes gleamed.

Michelle felt her muscles loosening and she laughed. "I never forgot yours, either, Larivière. Remember how I used to call you JP, the river?"

"We sure had a lot of fun with names, didn't we? Especially with Elphège--trying to find out if it meant anything special. Then we giggled and giggled as we tried to pronounce it in different ways. It didn't take much to get us into belly laughter!" JP's face took on the happy look of his boyhood. "I was only eight years old, but how well I remember that summer."

"And I was only seven," Michelle sighed. "Strange. It seems so long ago; and yet it seems like yesterday. So, tell me, how *did* you know that he's my father?"

"Two weeks ago, when I was assigned to work with a guy called 'El', I didn't think anything of it. Last week, however, when we were peeling potatoes, the supervisor called out, 'Bellerose, we need those spuds yesterday. Get with it!'

I stopped short and said, 'Oh, you're a Bellerose?'

'Ya. So what? Get going. They need the spuds!' he answered. So I got back to skinning the potatoes.

That night, alone in my cell, it suddenly came to me: Bellerose? El Bellerose? Could that be a nickname for Elphège? Then I thought, Oh no. That's too much of a coincidence. And even if it is the same name, it doesn't mean that he's her father. Forget it! But I could not.

So, the next day, I asked him if he knew a Michelle Bellerose. He stopped peeling, looked up and said, 'That's none of your business.'

'Hey! No big deal,' I told him, and went on, 'When I was a boy, I had a friend by that name in Canada. That's all.' As far as I was concerned, though, he had just answered 'Yes'.

I never mentioned it again until the day you came to visit him. We were in the exercise room and I overheard a guard tell him, 'So, your daughter's coming this afternoon!' Your father cast a swift glance in my direction, turned away and continued his push-ups. I was close to him, so in-between heaving my body up and down and struggling with my breathing, I sent a daring plea. 'I sure would like to see her again. Please tell her.'

He never looked my way. Just kept on with his exercises. That sapped my energy for the rest of the session."

"Sounds like my father, all right: Mr. Minus Personality.

"Well, I'm sure glad he changed his mind. I couldn't believe it when they told me you were coming. I haven't had a chance to thank him yet."

Michelle swished her hand. "Don't bother. Things aren't always what they seem."

"What do you mean?"

"Believe me, it's not important." *He just wanted to show me what kind of friends I have!*

"Whatever you say!" Then JP became very serious. "Michelle, I know that this might sound strange, but I *have* thought about you often. In Canada, we were young, it's true, but I never forgot all the fun we had together, and I'd sometimes wonder how you were. That's why I was so happy to hear about you. And that's why I wanted to see you. You made my day by coming."

"I'm really glad to see you, too," Michelle acknowledged sincerely.

"Now that you're here. . . I really had not planned to tell you this. . . but now I feel I want you to know it. If you don't believe me, I'll understand."

A frown of uncertainty gathered on Michelle's face and she began to feel uncomfortable. "It's okay, JP. You don't have to tell me anything. I know life can be crummy at times. I'm just glad to see you again."

"Michelle, look at me." He eyed her. "I won't blame you if you don't believe what I will tell you. After all, we really don't know one another very well. But what I say is true. I didn't do it. I did *not* rob or assault anyone."

Michelle gasped. "What!"

"I didn't do it. All I did was go in that store for a pack of cigarettes--and here I am." Once more, his eyes met hers directly.

Michelle almost choked. "I don't understand! Why are you here?"

"Two old ladies *and the victim* said that I was the only one there at the time. So, here I am--waiting to be tried for something I did *not* do."

Michelle's thinking went into high gear. "Well, first of all, can't you go out on bail?"

"I don't have that kind of money, and I never would ask my parents who are back in Canada. They have enough problems of their own and can just about pay their bills."

"I'll lend you the money. If you're not guilty, you shouldn't even be here. That's horrible."

"Thank you, but I can't accept that. Anyhow, the trial's just two weeks away."

"But ... "

His two palms rose and faced Michelle. "Please! That's not why I asked to see you. I just wanted to see you again and maybe reminisce a little."

She started to laugh. "About when we went looking for God?"

"What a day that was! I still remember how serious you were when you asked that man--Ivan--if he was God! Now there's another name that I didn't forget!"

"Did you ever find him?" Michelle asked.

"Find who?"

"God."

JP grinned. "I'm still trying. What about you?"

"I believe in God, and I go to church every week. But that belief is not what I was looking for that day. I was not looking for the "God" in God, the Father; I was looking for the "father" and the security of a father's love. I still remember the picture in that book. He looked so kind and good. That's what the picture meant to me."

"Wow. How'd you arrive at that conclusion?"

"That's a very long story. . . too long to start now. So, let's get back to you. Are you sure you don't want the bail money? I'm positive I can get some for you. Really."

"No. I've survived for nineteen years; I'll survive the next few weeks. Just say a prayer for me. The chaplain here says that helps. My parents were never church people, so I never learned much about God or things like that, but he says it doesn't matter. So I pray a lot." He paused. "Maybe you can get through better than me, though, so I would *really* appreciate your help."

"I'm *sure* the line's open for you as much as for me, but I'll keep your prayers company," Michelle promised heartily. She hesitated for a moment, then asked, "JP, tell me. What *did* happen?"

JP licked his lips. "I went in to buy cigarettes. While the clerk turned around to reach for them on a top shelf, I spotted a man, wearing sunglasses and a black jacket, crouched in one of the aisles. I thought he was looking for something on the lower level and wondered how in the world he could see with those dark glasses.

Then I paid for the cigarettes and ran out of the store because I was already late for work. While dashing out to my car, I shuffled the pack into the pocket of my black jacket and noticed a car chugging into the driveway. As I started the engine, in my rearview mirror, I saw that the white-haired woman in the long, blue Ford was waiting for me to back out before going into a parking space.

At 5:30 a.m. the next day, the doorbell woke me. I thought I had been dreaming until I heard it again. No one ever comes to see me at that time of day! So I jumped out of bed, rushed to the door and sneaked a peek through the peeping hole. It was the police! *What in the world do they want at this time of day?* I thought, as I finally opened the door. The next thing I knew, I was on my way to the police station where I found out that the store clerk was in the hospital after having been assaulted and robbed, and I was the chief suspect."

"My God! How horrible!" Michelle reached to touch his hand on the counter. "But how did they link that to you?"

"The two women saw me run out and they identified my car. How could they miss! It's a red and white Metro convertible."

"I see what you mean. Those cars stand out like a lead cheerleader in a parade. But how did they know it was yours?"

"While they were waiting for me to back out, one of them noticed my license number: 50005." He brushed the sweat from his brow and continued, "I got that plate because I thought it was cool to have an easy number to remember. How wrong I was!"

"But what about the other man you saw in the store? Didn't they see him?"

"They swear they did not. Supposedly, they just went in for cigarettes and headed straight to the cashier. They waited a few minutes, thinking that he was in the back room. Then they heard a slight groan behind the counter. Needless to say, the first woman who saw him on the floor almost passed out on top of him."

"I'll bet!"

"They thought he had fallen, so they called for help. When the ambulance arrived, however, the man was unconscious, and immediately the medics realized that he had been beaten by someone. They called the police.

By the time the police arrived, the two women were so hysterical that they had to be taken to the hospital; but not before the detectives got some information from them. That's when I became the prime suspect."

Michelle leaned forward. "Maybe they did it--those two women--or one of them—and then regretted it?"

"Not unless they were Amazons! He was killed by a couple of very forceful blows. Besides, they certainly wouldn't have stayed there to wait for the ambulance. I'm sure the police questioned them at length, but the evidence all zoomed onto me. So, here I am."

"So they saw your car. That doesn't mean *you* robbed and hurt someone?"

JP looked straight at her. "There's more. One said she saw me pushing something into my pocket when I ran out of the store. The assumption? I was hiding a gun or some other instrument.

Then it gets worse. The rest of the story comes from the victim himself. He said he was busy emptying a container and never actually saw me open the door and leave the store. Then, he heard something fall on the floor behind him, and as he turned to see what it was, the corner of his eye caught a black-sleeved arm. He remembers nothing after that. The police hauled away my black jacket, of course." Quick grin. "I hope they don't smoke Camels."

"How can you joke about this?"

"That's how I survive. Especially if it has a pinch or more of sarcasm in it. It's really more fun than depression."

"I'll think about that. So, what does your lawyer say about your case?"

"Not much, except that he'll do his best. I know he doesn't believe me, but I also know that he has represented a few local Mafia guys who got off easy. My conclusion? Guilty or not, he'll manage to keep me out of prison or keep the sentence at a minimum. That's what I'm counting on." His eyes met Michelle's. "It was him--or bail money. Couldn't have both."

"I wish I could do something to help you," Michelle said, "but I'm going back to New Hampshire at the end of this week. That's where I've been living since I left Canada."

"Here I am talking only about myself," JP apologized. "I never even asked how you're doing. I'm sorry."

"That's okay. I understand. I'm doing fine. In September I'll be starting school at Boston College. I'm really excited about that."

"That's great. I was studying to become a pharmacy assistant. Eventually, I was hoping to become a pharmacist. Wild dream, hey? Gee, maybe I can even become a prison pharmacist. Wouldn't that be something!"

Michelle could almost feel his pain and in her heart she wanted to believe his story, but the evidence against him was so clear that she didn't want to think about any of it right now. Instead, her thought turned to the future. *Guilty or not, he may end up in prison. And for a long time. I wonder. . .* She leaned forward and spoke softly. "JP, if you do go to prison, I'd be glad to write to you once in a while. May I?"

"Wow. Of course! You can't imagine what a pleasure it is to receive a letter in this place. My family's not much on writing. A letter from you would be a double pleasure."

"Great. I'll do that for you Larivière."

"Thanks Bellerose. If I do end up with a prison sentence, I sure will look forward to hearing from you. Thank you for caring."

She got up and looked at him ardently. "Good luck."

"Thanks. No matter what happens, I'll cherish this day forever." As he watched her walk away he made a visual recording of her to bring back to his cell. She was almost as tall as him, had a slim, well-proportioned body and long legs that were enhanced by her high-heeled shoes. Except for the blue ribbon that tied her long hair at the nape of the neck, she was dressed completely in a chic, white, marine-type outfit.

Her gait was slightly sexy, and her flared, white skirt swung in rhythm with every step. So did her bundled hair as it brushed against the wide, high-fashion "sailor collar" on her blouse.

At the exit, she stopped, turned and waved. Then she opened the door slowly and closed it gently.

In that instance, a surge of loneliness came over him. He slipped off his chair and thought: Now *I know that I love you, Michelle, and I know how futile that is.*

He turned and ambled sluggishly back to his cell.

Maybe Aunt Lena was right.

As she walked out, Michelle's thoughts jumped around in her head but never settled anywhere. *I can't get over this coincidence! I'll bet Aunt Lena would have a fit if she knew that I visited my father--and JP! Worse yet if she ever finds out that I promised to write to a prison inmate!*

The ride back home was tumultuous, as contradictory feelings of awe at the coincidence and helplessness with the event weakened her one moment and invigorated her the next.

The minute she got into the house, her mother said that Lena had called asking why Michelle had not phoned, as she promised she would. In any case, they would now come for her the next day.

"It's already time for you to leave!" Marie said sadly. "I'll miss you. You've been such a help-- especially with the boys. You know how to handle them better than I do."

"You know what to do now, Ma. We've talked about it enough, and we are starting to see results. Be *fair, fair and fair!* And encourage good behavior. Bad behavior sticks out; good behavior does not, unless it's exceptional. Find the every-day goodness in them, and don't be shy about letting them know that you see it and appreciate it. That'll encourage them, and they'll grow up. You'll see. In the meantime, please try not to get so upset about little things. Keep on telling yourself that it's not worth it. If you get sick, it won't help them or you."

"Easier said than done, but I'll do my best," Marie's tone emphasized the words. "Anyhow, I can't believe how mature you are. To think that I'm learning from my own daughter!"

Michelle shrugged it off. "We all learn from one another. I'm really concerned about you, though. I wish you could get out of here. . . go live near Grandmaman."

"Wild dream, Michelle. Your father would never let me sell this house. You know that!"

"Yep. When he gets out, he expects you and the house to welcome him with open arms and open doors. Don't be a fool, Ma. I can see that all he wants is someone to kiss his "a" and do his will. Sooner or later you have to get out of this trap."

"Don't call it that." Marie said sharply. "I know he has his bad side, but. . ."

"Bad side!" Michelle exclaimed. "We know that he raped at least one child, and was coming on to me--his own daughter; he drinks so much that now he's in jail for having maimed a boy; and he was in prison years back for having hurt someone with a beer bottle. He's got a violent temper." She paused. "Oh my goodness. Did he ever hurt you?"

"He never really harmed me."

"Is that the best you can do, Ma?"

"Yes. Your father has always been a good provider for the family. It's obvious that we're not rich, but we always had food on the table and heat in the winter. We even have our own home, which is more that a lot of people that I know." She paused. "We need him."

"*You* need him, Ma. Not me. And he needs you, too--to be his servant. But what about love? What about caring?"

"Dear child! That stuff doesn't last. I loved him, Michelle. And I know he loved me. Things have changed over the years. That's all. But I married him 'for better or for worse', and it's really not as bad as you think. Sure, he's a little rough at times, but he knows when to get out of the house."

"I'm sorry, but *I don't believe that*. He doesn't care for anyone but himself. He doesn't even seem to regret what he did to that boy! He just wants to use you, and you don't see it. Maybe Aunt Lena was right."

"Stop that! Leave Lena out of this! Finishing high school doesn't make her a know-it-all, although that's what she thinks she is. And now that she has that big title, all she does is talk like a snob. She makes me feel like I'm nothing."

Michelle went over to hug her. "Come on, Ma. She just doesn't understand. She's ten years younger than you. In those days ten years made a *big* difference in the attitude toward education."

"I know, honey. That's why I want you to go to college. Everything that I didn't have--and more--I want for you. And I promise I'll write to you more often, even though I'm not good at it."

"Thanks, Ma. I'll be waiting for your letters."

"After all I did for you, you do this to me!"

Michelle did not sleep all night. In bed, she swished from one position to another, and her mind kept racing. Everything and everyone jutted in and out of her consciousness: her mother, her father, Jean Paul, her brothers, Aunt Lena. They all kept going under and resurfacing like drowning persons coming up for air. And somehow, in some way, she felt that *she was the air.*

Around 4:30 a.m. she got up, made coffee and sat in the living room, drinking from the cup sip by sip and yearning for dawn to come. An hour later, she saw it creeping up behind the horizon. She had emptied her cup. Slowly, she rose, went to the sink to rinse it, and then returned to her bedroom to get dressed. She had faced the dawn; now she had to get ready to face the day.

At breakfast time, she put on her sunny-side-up face, but she overestimated her ability to hide her feelings, especially from her mother. By the time Jean left for work and David ran out to play, Marie could see behind the mask. She looked straight at her daughter and said, "I know something's bothering you. What's wrong?"

"Oh no, Ma. Not at all. I've just been thinking about a lot of things. . . and I've made up my mind. Aunt Lena will be so hurt and upset."

"Her again! What in the world could you say that would upset her?"

"I'm *staying here*, Ma. I'm not going back to Oakton, and I'm not going to college in Boston."

Boom!

Marie fell onto the nearest chair. "She won't be upset, Michelle. She'll be on fire. You can't do that!"

"Yes, I can. I've prayed a lot about this. This is what I want to do, *at least for this year.*"

"But why? I'll learn to live without El in the house. I'll manage. You'll see!"

"I love you, Ma. I just want some time to help you get on your feet."

"But, honey, you were going to a fancy college. You can't just quit that."

"Right now my family's more important than a degree in a fancy school. Who cares! Except Aunt Lena. I can get a good education right here in Vermont. Besides, if I want to, I can transfer to Boston next year."

"I don't know what to say, Michelle. I sure wasn't expecting this. It's such a wonderful surprise. But it also makes me very uncomfortable."

"Believe me, this was *not* in my plans. It's a surprise to me as well. Anyhow, now I have to call Aunt Lena before they get in the car."

Marie's ashen face frowned anxiously. "Honey, are you sure you really want to do this? I don't feel right about this. Lena will surely think that I encouraged this."

"Ma, stop your worrying. It's not your decision; it's mine. And that's what I want to do. Okay? Now smile so that I can have support when I tell your sister." She went to the phone, picked up the handset and dialed.

Marie's faint smile couldn't cover her anxiety.

When she heard Lena's voice, Michelle could feel sweat flood her underarms. She took a deep breath and excitedly said, "Hi, Auntie."

"Michelle? We were just getting ready to leave. What's up?"

Michelle gulped. "Auntie, I have something to tell you."

Marie sat in her chair, her praying lips going a mile a minute.

"Oh God! Well, whatever happened now. Are you telling me you're still not ready?"

Michelle brushed her hair away from her forehead. "I'm sorry, but … "

"But what?"

Michelle counted: one, two, three, go and raced her words through the phone line. "I made a big decision. I'm staying here. I won't be going to college in Boston."

"What!" The scream almost burst Michelle's ear drums.

"I'm staying here, with my mother for a year--*just one year*. I'll go to college in Montpelier."

"Are you crazy? You've already been accepted in Boston! Who put that in your mind? Your mother? Let me talk to her!"

"My mother had *nothing* to do with this. In fact, she told me *not* to do it. But I've thought a lot about it, and I've prayed a lot, and I've made up my mind."

"Let me speak to Marie!" she hollered so loudly that Marie heard her from across the room.

"No. She has *nothing* to do with this. Nothing at all." Silence. . . "I'm sorry. I don't want to hurt you. I just have to do this." Her voice quivered, but her hand tightened around the phone. "I'll write and tell them I've changed my mind."

"After all that I did for you, you do this to me!" Lena shrieked. "I've given you the kind of life you could only have dreamed of, and you turn around and tell me you'd rather stay up there in the sticks and go to an inferior college! I can't believe it!"

"Please, Auntie! I am *so very grateful* to you. I really mean it. But it's just for a year. I'm sure it won't take longer than that to settle things around here, and I can transfer to Boston next year.

"That's stupid!" Pause. "Leo! Damn it, he's not here! Listen, Michelle, don't listen to your mother. It'll ruin your life!" Silence. "Michelle!"

Michelle lowered her voice and spoke carefully. "I just want you to calm down before I say anything else. I repeat: My mother had *nothing* to do with this. She said that I should *not* do it. But I thought about it a lot, and it's what I want to do. I'm *not* ruining my life. I *will* go to college, get my degree and get a good job. I'm just going to do it in a different way. . . Aunt Lena!. . . She hung up."

Slowly she closed the telephone and went to her mother. "The next call should be from Leo."

Marie's hand swung up to her lips. "Oh, my God, what's going to happen now!"

"Stop worrying, Ma. Smile and enjoy the day. Believe me, the worse is over."

An hour later, Leo was on the line. Michelle could hear Lena whispering to him, but it was to no avail. She was not changing her mind. So, he ended the conversation, wished her luck and insisted that she call often to let them know how things were working out.

Just before they hung up, Michelle heard Lena sobbing in the background. She couldn't believe it, and as she replaced the handset a crushing feeling of guilt hit her and pushed her onto the nearest chair. For a moment, she felt like joining Lena's tears, but she did not. Instead, she said a short prayer for her aunt, and then turned her thoughts to another major decision: when and how to tell her brothers that she would be here for another year. She decided on suppertime.

That evening, while Jean and David were gobbling their homemade chocolate pudding, Michelle gave them the news. "I have something to tell you guys."

Their eyes went up, as they kept eating.

"I'm not going back to Oakton. I'm staying here for another year at least and will go to college in Montpelier."

Jean responded very positively. His fears that Michelle would replace him had been dissipating little by little and now he told her that he was glad to have her around to help out. David was not overjoyed, but showed no resistance. Deep down, he was beginning to like his sister who always encouraged him in his endeavors and even stood up for him at times.

This unexpected, pleasant surprise was like a salve on her anxiety, and immediately her appetite for her mother's creamy pudding drew her to a second helping.

As she was enjoying her dessert, however, her mind wandered to another hurdle: what to do about JP. *Should I say something about him now? Or later? Or at all?* She struggled with this for a couple hours and finally, when everyone was home and quietly focused on their own evening tidbits, she opened her next box of surprises. "I visited another inmate at the prison. He's a friend of mine from way back."

"Ouch!" Marie jerked her mending needle out of her finger, Jean dropped his comic book, and David's mouth stuck open.

Marie thumb-trapped the dot of blood on her finger. "What are you saying?"

Michelle explained how she had met JP in Canada, and then again at the prison. As soon as she told them that he was arrested for robbery and assault, Jean interrupted her.

"Are you talking about the Larivière who beat up the store clerk?"

"Yes."

"You know *him*? Wow! He then went on to say how he had heard all about him at the barber shop. One of the customers knew the victim well and the crime had been on everyone's tongue the whole time he was having his hair cut. "I hope you don't go visit him again. He's violent--just like our father."

"Hey!" David cried out. "Our father was drunk. He wasn't robbing anybody!"

Michelle intervened before any other word came out. "Come on, boys. Things aren't always what they seem. In fact, JP told me that he did *not* do it."

"Ha, ha, ha," Jean's mocking laughter filled the air. "And you believe it? Really, Michelle, I thought you were smarter than that!"

"Hey, I don't know whether he's guilty or not, but in the USA a person is innocent until proven guilty. Right?" she emphasized. "He has *not* been tried and convicted yet. So maybe we should all be a little less judgmental."

Marie looked at both boys. "She's right."

Jean could not stop. "He was only eight years old when you knew him. A lot of things have happened between then and now. Just look at *our* family!"

Michelle's eyes wandered out the window and into the distant horizon. "I know, but something tells me that he's telling the truth. It's a kind of intuition."

"You women and your intuition! I hope a woman is never elected president. Can you imagine what would happen? Anyhow, right now you're the one that's getting involved, and I don't like it. You'll get into trouble."

"Come on, Jean. I'm not doing anything, except planning to go to the trial." *And writing to him.*

"Did you hear that, Ma? She's going to the trial!" His hands went flying. "Whatever! If that's what you want! But don't faint when you hear the verdict. No one will be there to catch you." He put away his comics. "Come on, David, it's getting late, and we both have to get up early tomorrow."

David didn't look up. "I wanna finish my crossword puzzle."

Jean rolled his eyes. "You can finish it in your bedroom. Come on."

David got up slowly. "I can't wait to be an adult!" He followed Jean up the stairs.

He must be so damned scared.

A few days before JP's trial, Michelle visited him again. She wanted him to know that someone cared, and that she would be at his trial. The minute she saw him, however, she realized that her feelings for him ran much deeper than she wanted. Even in his dull prison garb, he looked marvelous, sexy, appealing. He sat down and when he greeted her, she was amazed at how the high-pitched voice of his childhood days had changed into such a pleasing and comforting sound.

"I can't believe this," he said, as he pulled out his chair." What a nice and unexpected surprise. How are you?"

"I'm fine. I just wanted to tell you that I'd like to come to your trial, if it's okay with you."

"Of course it's okay. But why? I know how busy you are at home."

He must be so damned scared. Yet, here he is concerned about me. "I know that none of your family can be here, so I think you should have at least one supporter: me."

He barricaded tears. "Thanks."

The hour passed very quickly, and at its end, Michelle's intuition still told her that he was not guilty. Or was it more than intuition? *This is insane,* she thought. *I like him too much; I'd like to hug him right now. It's really insane! What if he is a violent person? What if he is guilty? What's happening to me!*

The conversation had remained in neutral, however. In an attempt to stifle their fears, at least for the moment, they had talked about everyday stuff. But all the while, running persistently and gnawingly underneath the small talk was the fact that in a few days JP's life would be fated for better--or for worse.

Finally, it was time to leave. Michelle got up reluctantly. "I'll be there," she told him, "and I'll be praying for a miracle."

"Thank you. I'll need one."

Michelle paused for a moment. Then she waved goodbye and walked slowly to the exit.

JP could not watch her leave. He rose quickly and hurried away.

"I wanted to change, but I felt I was too far gone."

The next Monday, Michelle drove down to Vermont College. When she finally rolled into a parking space near the Administration Building, her thoughts were racing. *What if the slots are all filled up? What if I can't get into a degree program? Every day counts. I should have come before Stop it! Think positive!*

She took a last look at herself in the rearview mirror, pushed back her hair and grabbed her bag--one so huge that it could carry and conceal not only her keys and female minutia, but also transcripts and other information that she needed to enroll in this institution.

As she was going up the long path to the Administration Office, she noticed an old man, his back to her, watering the late-summer flowers that were blooming beautifully in one of the gardens next to the building. His denim overalls seemed a little too big for him, but his poppy-red T-shirt clung to him tightly. He seemed completely focused, as his white head followed the hose that he was swishing back and forth over the garden.

Just as she was going up the steps of the building, she felt mist on her arm and turned around to face the gardener. Her heart skipped a few beats.

"I'm sorry, Miss," the man apologized, "I didn't get you wet, did I? Sometimes it sprays farther than I expect."

"That's okay. It was just a few drops." She stayed still, staring at him.

"Good." Her gaze made him feel uncomfortable and he quickly returned to his watering.

Michelle went down and walked up to him. "Ivan?"

"Yes." The man turned quickly.

"I can't believe this. You're Ivan?"

"Yes. You know me?" All the lines on his face crinkled questioningly.

"I'm Michelle--Michelle Bellerose. I'm the girl that thought you were God. Remember?"

"Damn it! I would never have recognized you. You're all grown up!"

"Well, I recognized you right away! How could I miss that white hair and beard! I surely *never* expected to see you again, though. How are you?"

"I'm fine. In fact, thanks to you and that boy you were with." He shut off the hose.

"That was JP Larivière. What do you mean?"

"For one thing, your question went right down to my laughing belly. I hadn't laughed in months, and it really felt good. Then, of course, everything else happened, and I thought: I can change. Yes, I can."

Michelle looked at him quizzically. "I don't under-stand."

"My dear girl, I had been in and out of prison since I was seventeen. The last time for ten years. I had been released just a few weeks before I met you, and I wasn't even supposed to be in Canada. But I have connections, and I wanted to visit my Canadian cousin, so I went in illegally."

"Oh, you're American?"

"Yes. Anyhow, after those last ten years of doing time, I had had it! When I walked out of there I was so damned mad at myself that I cried because of what I had done with my life: I had wasted all those years. Worse yet, I had hurt many along the way. It took forty-five years for my brain to accept those facts, and now, instead of giving me peace because I faced the truth, it was pulverizing me. *Scum I am and scum I will always be. Who the hell's gonna hire you? You hate yourself, you hate the world. That's what scums do,* I thought, and I started to throw things around the shitty room that I had rented with the very few bucks I made in prison. That's when I decided I had to get away for a few days to clear my head. So I decided to visit my cousin. We grew up together and he's the only one in the family who talks to me.

Two days later, I met you kids and within a few minutes three unusual things happened: you asked me that innocent but incredulous question, I saved a child from drowning, and --I'll always remember that little-girl voice of yours--you said, 'You saved him. You're like God'.

A few minutes later, the two of you ran right out of my life, but the events had not. When I went back home, I couldn't get those things out of my mind. They were like an obsession until I sat down one day and realized that, somehow, they were linked. As a whole, they became a message: God -save a child -you are like God. Something happened to me at that moment. In a flash, I knew for sure that I *could* rise from the mire; I could change, I could have a new beginning, I could help others instead of hurting them, I could be at peace.

That night, for the very first time in my life, I sincerely prayed for help.

It hasn't been easy, but here I am, more at peace and more content than ever. I've been working here for over ten years now, and I love it."

Stirred by this unexpected revelation, Michelle went to hug him. "I don't know what to say! This is unbelievable. I'm so happy for you. You really look great."

He cupped her hand in his. "And how are *you*--and JP? Do you ever hear from him?"

Michelle's face faded. "I guess you don't know. JP's in the state prison here in Vermont."

"Oh no! What happened?" He let go of Michelle and instinctively brushed his beard.

"It's a very long story, but I'll make it short," she started.

When she finished Ivan was nodding in agreement with her. "I do remember hearing about that robbery, not from the newspaper, though. I don't buy it. It was at the club where I hang out a few times a week. Now that I think of it, they kept referring to the guy as "Larivière", but they never mentioned his first name. "I'm so sorry."

She became very pensive. "Going to prison for something you did is one thing; but to be imprisoned when you did nothing wrong is quite another. Imagine, living in a prison cell for years and years and knowing that you're innocent. That must affect you for life."

Ivan touched her shoulder. "Don't give up hope. No matter what they found, he may be telling the truth. I know how it is. I lived with prisoners who were innocent. Unfortunately, the jury had not believed them." His lips bonded tightly and he nodded sadly.

"Well, I'm not sure, of course. I just feel it deep inside. It's an intuition. I wish I could help him."

"Ah yes. Women and their intuition! That won't be much help now, I'm afraid. His trial is next Thursday?"

"Yes, I went to see him last week, and I'll go to the trial. He doesn't have family around here anymore."

"That's mighty good of you. I'm sure he needs all the support he can get."

Michelle checked her watch. "Oh my, I'll be late for my appointment. I'm so glad to have seen you again.

Gee, I already know someone on this campus! Maybe it's a good sign! In any case, I'm sure we'll meet again. Bye."

Ivan waved and watched her as she hop-skipped up the stairs and into the building.

The press went wild. What had just happened?

Finally, Thursday arrived. Michelle was one of the first persons to get into the courtroom. She looked around in awe. *This is the place of judgment, the place where one person's life is held in the hands of a few.* The solemnity of it gave her goose bumps, and a feeling of depression came over her as she surveyed the environment. Everything in it was dark except the white walls and the light that slid through the two small, high widows and landed directly on the judge's ornate mahogany dais and furnishings.

Finally, she took a seat on one of the long benches in the spectator section and watched with curiosity as members of the press and radio stations came in with all their paraphernalia and settled in their reserved space. Several other persons came In haphazardly and a few of them made their way to the bench in front of her. Eventually, the group grew to five and their conversation revealed that they did this as a hobby. They were chatting, laughing and opining about the outcome of the trial. "That guy's guilty" was the expressed conclusion of each of them. In fact, one of them even suggested that they might as well go home because they were wasting time here; they already knew what would happen.

But another said that the victim was his neighbor, and he saw how brutally he had been hurt. He wanted to stay and have the satisfaction of seeing JP's face when the jury condemns him. Everyone in the clique agreed, so they all remained.

Every word coming out of their mouth was like a knife-stab to Michelle and she tensed up, struggling to stop *her* words from leaving her mouth. After a few minutes, she began to breathe slowly, in and out, in and out. . .

Then, someone tapped her on the shoulder. She turned to see Ivan motioning her to move over so that he could sit next to her.

"I noticed how disturbed you were the other day," he whispered. "I asked for time off from work to come with you."

She smiled appreciatively. "Thank you so much."

As she was saying this, the lawyers came in, followed by JP, handcuffed and led by a guard. He glanced toward the audience and saw Michelle. Their eyes met. Michelle froze with fear. *What if he's not guilty, but is convicted? What if he is guilty? Why do I feel that he's telling me the truth? Why am I wishing it?*

Then the bailiff came in and almost roared, "All stand. His Honorable Judge McKinley."

The judge, his black robe flowing with his quick steps, took his place like an actor on stage, perused through a few papers and looked up and around the room.

Everyone was in place. The trial began.

Jeb Sawyer, the prosecuting attorney was grandiose and eloquent. After all, the reporters from various newspapers and radio stations were avidly waiting to guzzle up every bit of information they could get, and by so doing, possibly make him famous.

The two aged witnesses had surely recovered from their original hysteria. They were powdered and primped to go on stage, and if they had been panicky about having to go on the stand, it did not show during this interrogation. Atty. Sawyer slickly worded his way into their hearts, and they felt quite at ease and ready to explain the horror of their discovery. One of the women, in fact, seemed to be enjoying her notoriety so much that she kept on smiling and looking around, even while describing the ugly events of that fateful day. The lawyer had to keep on refocusing her, and each time he did, she returned to the moment with more damaging information.

The defense attorney, Eddy Finstein, was not so lucky, at least not with the first witness. Try as he might, his words and mannerisms simply drew from her a sourpuss countenance and blunt answers, neither of which added any favor to JP's case.

Then the second woman was called. She swore on the Bible, sat down and pressed her lips tightly, even before the lawyer started to question her. Atty. Finstein approached, looked at her as kindly as he could fake it and opened his mouth, but before any sound could hit the air, jumbled mumblings rattled through the room. A young man had come in from the side door and handed a paper to the bailiff who, in turn, brought it to the judge.

For a moment, the judge seemed upset, but as he read the note, his face turned into full surprise. He called the two lawyers to the bench and read the message to them. They looked at one another in astonishment and returned to their place.

Then the judge addressed the jurors. "Ladies and gentlemen of the jury, we will take a recess for a few minutes." He got up and waved to the attorneys. "Lawyers and prisoner, please come to my chamber."

The press went wild. What had just happened? Would someone--anyone--give them information? It was frenzy at its best.

Michelle, however, was so stunned that she could not move. Ivan took her by the arm. "Let's go outside for a while." He lifted her.

"What happened?"

Ivan didn't answer right away. He led her out of the courtroom, and as they entered into the open, spacious lobby, he tried to comfort her. "We have to wait. This is just a recess. Surely something very important has happened, though. Hopefully it's something in JP's favor. What do you think?"

Michelle sighed. "Right now I can't think of anything. I don't know if I can take anymore waiting, though. Sometimes, that's worse than knowing. What in the world could have happened?"

A few seconds later, the guard in the lobby said that recess had ended and he signaled them to go back in, but they never had a chance to do so. As soon as they reached the open door, a reporter ran by, waving his arms and exclaiming excitedly to them, "I can't believe it. This guy didn't do it!"

A second one bumped into Ivan. "Wait till I get to my editor!"

Inside, the judge was talking to the jurors, but the three men and two women who had been sitting in front of Michelle got up and walked out. "Something's wrong here," one of them was saying, "This guy has to be guilty. Somebody must have gotten paid off."

Michelle hobbled over to the nearest bench and dropped on it. "Did I hear right? He's *not* guilty? How do they know? Is this for real?"

"I guess it is," Ivan said, his eyes gleaming with excitement. "How wonderful." He looked at his watch. "Well, it's over, Michelle. I have to go back now. You can tell me all about it later. Please tell JP that I'm super happy for him." He waved goodbye and hurried away.

Michelle waved back. "See you later. Thanks for coming."

Then she saw JP and a sheriff turning around the corner in the hallway. He was not handcuffed anymore, and when he noticed her, he said something to the guard and started towards her. She didn't wait. She ran to him and they hugged until they were almost breathless.

When they finally unhooked, her first question was, "What happened?"

"It's kind of a miracle, I guess," he said, "About a half hour ago, they got a signed confession from the person who did it."

"You're kidding me!" Her two hands met in a clap and her astonished countenance sparkled.

"No, it's true! Remember? I told you that there *was* someone else in that store. They call him BBen. He was a former employee. When he heard the old lady's car, he knew he had to move fast, so he threw a chocolate bar behind the clerk, who turned around to see what had happened. At that moment, BBen jumped forward and crashed an iron bar on his head. Within a minute, he opened the register, grabbed the money and ran to the cellar. Just as he closed that door, he heard the women come into the store.

Luck was with him. The cellar bunker was unlocked. He dashed out into the back yard and headed for the woods behind the store. The women had not seen him, and the clerk had never seen his face.

"That's unbelievable!" she said, "So how did they finally catch him?"

"All I know right now is that, at the last minute, something came up that linked him to the crime and they had no trouble finding him because he was already in prison. I still can't believe it!"

"It's like a miracle," Michelle said animatedly. "I'm so happy for you!"

He took her hand in his own two. "Thank you so much for coming." He paused briefly. "Well, I have to go back to the prison. There's a lot of paperwork to be done, but I'll be out soon."

"I really wanted to be there for you," was all that Michelle said, but her eyes were pleading.

This didn't get past JP. "Do you suppose we could meet again?"

"Yes, of course. Here, I'll give you my telephone number." Digging into her large pocketbook, she found a sales receipt and quickly jotted down her number. Then she remembered Ivan. "Call me soon. I have so much to tell you. And I'm eager to find out more about what happened."

To their disappointment, however, the complete story would not be known until many years later.

"At that moment I became aware of God."

Two weeks later, JP was back at his former job and his Metro had been returned to him. He took advantage of his first "day off" to drive Michelle to school and to meet Ivan. Since she had told him about their mysterious friend, JP had been eager to see him again.

Although she had not been able to get all the required courses for her first semester, she had managed to get into two of them. Both started that afternoon and JP went to the library to read while he waited for her. A few hours later, she walked in, all excited about her new adventure: college. She hardly stopped talking as they left and walked out to keep their appointment with Ivan.

As soon as he saw them, he jaunted across the lawn and waved heartily. Jean Paul's memory jolted back to that summer day in Canada, and he hurried to meet the aged man, whose hand was extended to meet his. They stayed in a warm, steady handshake for a few minutes. "How well I remember the day we met you," JP exclaimed.

"So do I. How could I forget! Two kids thinking that I was God!" Ivan's white beard followed his lips in a wide smile.

"Well, to me you did look like him!" Michelle said in raillery.

"To tell the truth," JP confessed, "I wasn't sure what we were looking for, but I went along with Michelle. That's what she did to me, even then!"

Ivan winked at Michelle.

But Michelle didn't notice. She was wrapped in her pensive mode. "When I moved to Aunt Lena's, I forgot all about that day. It's not till much later that I remembered it and realized that I had not been looking for God, but for the security of a father's love. Then the strangest thing happened. At that moment, I *really* became aware of God."

"You talk in mysteries, Mademoiselle," JP quipped. "I thought you found him in church every week. Is there more than one God?"

Michelle nudged his arm with her elbow. "Come on! You know what I mean. It was an experience rather than a thought."

JP shrugged his shoulders and looked at Ivan. "I have no idea what you're talking about."

"Well, maybe you *don't* understand," she mumbled and continued, "I'm serious. After talking to my father a few weeks ago, I left the prison angrier than when I went in.

On the way home, I realized that I did *not* want to be angry for the rest of my life, and I decided that my 'wishful father image' had done enough damage. I *had* to let go of it and accept him 'as is', but I felt that I couldn't handle that by myself. So I said, 'God, please help both of us. I hand him over to you for his good and mine.'

In *that* instance, I became aware of a loving Presence that I knew to be the God in 'God, the Father' He was no longer a father image, no longer a thought, but something beyond all that--a mysterious and awesome Presence breathing all into existence, nurturing all--as in a mother's womb. And I realized that I had *never* been alone, or without nurturing and protective love. Then a peace such as I never felt filled my very being." She nodded to JP. "That's the best way that I can explain it."

Ivan's eyes mirrored his pondering. "How well I understand. When I met you two in the park, I had given up on myself. In my mind, I would always be scum.

Then, when I went home and thought about everything that had happened, I began to see it as a message from God that I *could* change because, deep down I was good, not bad.

No one had ever said that to me, but in that moment I knew it was the truth. In his own mysterious way, God was helping me to discover my real self. That's when I realized that, even in my destructive days, even when I didn't want him around, *He was there* waiting. When I crashed at the bottom of the pit, I finally stopped and listened."

Michelle smiled. "It does start with listening, but it looks to me as if you did more than that. You took action."

"I must admit, it wasn't easy. In fact, I went back to the prison to see the chaplain. Was he ever surprised! We talked for a long time and I went home realizing that the first thing I had to do was change my thinking. I had to start seeing life, people, and things from a different perspective, so I started to read from the Bible and other books of spirituality. Even when things got really tough, I never lost hope. Now I am at peace and I thank God every day.

"Isn't that wonderful, JP?" Michelle exclaimed. Then, to Ivan, "*You* gave me hope, too. When you told me your story, immediately I thought about my father.

Who knows? Maybe one day he'll meet his truth, too. I hope so."

By now JP was really fascinated. "You won't believe this, but just a while ago, at the library, I came across this quotation from St. Paul: 'For in him we live and move and have our being, as even some of your poets have said.' I couldn't quite figure it out, but now I think I'm beginning to understand. This is awesome."

"And now I'm beginning to get hungry!" Michelle chuckled and tugged at JP's jacket. "Let's go, or we'll be late for our dinner reservations. You know how I feel about punctuality!"

"Do I!" JP attested as his eyes rolled and stopped on Ivan. "Come. We've got a lot of catching up to do." He grabbed Michelle's hand and they all hurried to the car like a bunch of kids going to the beach.

"Anyhow, I'm glad that you're the first to know."

At the restaurant they were able to get a table near a window view of the distant, awesome mountains of Vermont that were changing little by little in the dimming light of the vanishing sun. Their initial excitement about the grandeur of that landscape did not last long, however. They were soon talking about their individual lives, and for a few hours, they sat, sharing their experiences of the past and imagining those of the future.

Then, just before they left, JP surprised Michelle. "I have something for you," he said, as he dug into his jacket pocket, took Michelle's hand and placed a small box in her palm.

Michelle's wide eyes gravitated to the tiny, tastefully-wrapped package. She was so surprised that all she said was "What's that?"

116

"What a question to ask!" He winked at Ivan and returned his gaze to Michelle. "Just open it and you'll see!"

Cautiously and a little shakily, Michelle opened it and a gold chain peeked out of the inner wrapping. As she lifted it, a gold ring adorned with a dark red garnet surrounded by tiny diamonds sparkled in the light of the candle that had been burning at their table.

"It's your birthstone," JP informed her, "But more so, it was my mom's birthstone, too. . . *and* her pre-engagement ring. I kept it all these years--waiting for the right person and the right moment."

Michelle's hand was getting shaky. "Can I wear it now?"

"Of course you can--and you *may*," JP jested. "Here, let me help you." He took the chain, pulled out the ring and placed it on her finger. Then he hooped the long necklace around her head, and when it settled on her chest, he gazed at her in silence--until Cupid stopped dancing in his heart. Finally, he found his voice again. "Looks awesome!"

"Thank you." Silence. Cupid had reached her, too! Everything was still, except the heartbeats.

Ivan started to feel like a third party, but he really didn't mind. After a few minutes, however, he lifted his glass of wine and jarred them out of their romantic coma by a loud and cheerful "Congratulations to both of you."

They returned to earth.

"I'm sorry," JP apologized. "This ring has been in my pocket for three days, but I hadn't planned to give it to her tonight. But there's something about this place. . . maybe the candle light, or the ambiance, or. . . Anyhow, I started to feel it burning in my pocket."

Ivan laughed. "Maybe I look like Father Time and you felt pressured? You know. . . The long, white beard and everything. Though I must say, mine is not as long as his!"

"That's it! It was pressure from you that drove me to this!"

A few guffaws from the men and a muted laugh from Michelle followed. Consciously or not, she was still under Aunt Lena's rule: "We never talk or laugh loud in a restaurant. It's not polite."

When the giggling ended, she looked at Ivan. "I'm glad that you're the first to know. Somehow it seems very appropriate."

"Thank you," Ivan grinned and raised his wine glass.

Then the three glasses kissed and their happy clink recorded in everyone's memory as a night of dawning love and lifetime friendship.

CHAPTER 7

"But how did he find what the police could not?"

Five years later, JP, who was now a registered pharmacist, Michelle, and their baby boy who had just been baptized the day before visited Ivan who was wheelchair bound and living in a nursing home.

They had rolled him into the visitor's lounge and for a while much of the chit chat was about Michelle and her family.

Michelle had just received her degree from Vermont College, and she was anticipating an interview for a part-time teaching job in the local elementary school. She opted for job sharing rather than full-time because she wanted to be with her baby as much as possible.

Ivan was amazed that she had been able to finish college, get married and have a baby in so short a period. He obviously had never met her mentor, Aunt Lena.

Lena, of course, had been very hurt by Michelle's decision to stay with her mother, but eventually she accepted it. She wasn't about to be left childless, however. Auntie never gave up. She got pregnant and now, several times a year she and Leo drive up to Mapleview to show off their new daughter, always dressed in very chic baby clothes and smelling as sweet as a. . . whatever! Baby perfume was now Aunt Lena's newest craze.

All the boys, except Jean and David were married and doing fine. Jean had his own apartment and he was skimming the edge of marriage. David was still living at home. He had earned a scholarship to attend the community college that had just been built in the next town. Three days a week, he bussed to the campus for his classes. The other two days, he worked in Bellini's Market to earn money for board and personal expenses.

Her father was still in prison, but he had softened somewhat under the influence of Marie and David. Chauffeured by Jean, who now owned a car, they went to see El regularly. Jean usually waited in another room. He had gone to see his father a couple of times, but it always turned out to be more disturbing than not, and he preferred to stay away.

At the beginning, the visits were difficult even for Marie and David. Elphège was curt, rude and distant. After several meetings, Marie detected strong, undercover feelings of guilt and embarrassment in her husband, and she thought that his macho rudeness was his way of keeping these feelings out of sight, and especially out of *his own* sight. So she tried very hard not to react so much or so angrily when he was callous and crude.

As time went on, he began to speak more openly about his feelings, and the visitation tensions diminished. It took several months, but eventually he was actually looking forward to seeing his family.

It was Marie, however, who was the gem in the surprise box. She was now feeling very well and was employed full time in a flower shop, where her floral arrangements were in constant demand. Every day she thanked God for Michelle who stayed with her and led her gently out of unhealthy dependence and into self sufficiency.

She did *not* need Elphège anymore, but she continued to visit him. . . and often thought about the early days with him when they were so much in love. Time had brought about disturbing changes, however and, married or not, she did not know if she could ever live with him again. That was for the future to decide.

Then, somehow, the conversation reverted to earlier times and to the day of JP's freedom.

"I wonder why that private investigator got involved with my case?" JP was really perplexed. "I could never have afforded him." Then his eyes rounded in a moment of enlightenment and he turned to Michelle. "I never thought of it! The only one who could have afforded him was you!"

Instantaneously, Michelle's thumb went to her chest. "No. Cross my heart! That never even came to my mind. Gee, JP, if I had done that, I surely would have told you before now!"

The spark in his eyes dimmed, and he mumbled, "You're right. But who. . ."

Ivan leaned forward in his chair and said softly, "I think I know who did it."

Michelle's eyes widened. "You do?"

Astonished, JP reversed the question. "Do you?"

Ivan was chuckling inside. "Come closer. I don't want to say it too loudly."

The couple looked at one another. Then, Michelle, baby and JP approached the man who remained silent.

"Well, who did it?" JP asked.

"I did."

Michelle almost shrieked, "What?"

JP was speechless.

Ivan shrugged his shoulders and let the moment be itself.

Finally, JP found his voice again. "Why?. . You could afford him?"

Ivan's palm swished upward. "First of all, let me explain something. I *could not* say a word about it because, at the time, I was an active informant. That investigator, Simon, was the best--and he owed me. When I asked him to help, he hesitated because the trial was just a few days away. But I convinced him that he might feel pretty bad about himself if he had not tried and later on found out that you were *not* guilty."

JP's lines of bewilderment made their appearance again. "But how did he find what the police could not? I thought they had done a thorough investigation."

"They did, but they missed something: a glass lens."

"A glass lens?" Michelle's voice was now above high C.

"Here's what I was told. When BBen ran into the cellar, it was dark and as he pulled off his sunglasses, he dropped them on the floor and one of the glasses broke. Instinctively, he picked up the frame and sped out, leaving behind a big piece of the broken lens. Of course, as soon as he noticed the damaged glasses, he ditched them.

The police had looked in the cellar, but not thoroughly enough, I suppose. Probably for several reasons: First, there were no fingerprints on the cellar doorknob, except the clerk's. BBen had worn gloves and had grabbed only the edges of the knob, thereby leaving the clerk's fingerprints all over it, and none of his own. Secondly, they already had two credible witnesses insisting that a man with a black jacket had run out of the store. To top it all, there was the victim who said that, as soon as he gave you your change, he got back to unloading stock and never actually saw you leave the store. Moreover, he insisted that he had seen something like a black sleeve just before he was hit. He remembered that you had a black jacket. It seemed to be a clear-cut case.

So, when Simon, went to investigate, the store owner was not too pleased. As far as he was concerned, this was a closed case, and he didn't want anymore interference in his business. He conceded, however, when a couple of green bills flashed before him.

Well, as I said before, 'nothing escapes Simon'. About twenty minutes into his prying, he came upon pieces of a broken beer bottle, and about an inch from that pile, a piece of dark glass that didn't match anything in that area. He picked it up very carefully by the sides and realized that it was a sunglass lens. Immediately he remembered that you had seen a man with sunglasses in the store. He completed his search and then, on the wildest of wild hopes, he used his illegal siren and rushed to the police station.

Once more he found resistance, but his investigative reputation won out and the police finally rushed the piece of glass to the lab.

The rest is history. They found BBen's fingerprint on it and they had no trouble finding him because he was already in jail for another robbery." He looked at JP, "He confessed as you were walking into the courtroom."

"It's a miracle!" Michelle said in amazement, as she looked at Ivan. "It's as if you, Simon and the others involved were inspired and driven to work on finding the truth. And the fact that you succeeded at the very last minute is nothing short of miracle."

"Call it what you want," Ivan's voice trembled a bit. "I call it God's love.

"Amen," JP and Michelle said in unison, "Amen."

Then, Michelle changed to her "pensive mode", and everyone waited.

"You know what's most interesting about all this?" she said almost mysteriously. "The road to truth, for each of us, has been very long and amazingly. . . it all began with the family secret."

In the moment that followed, even the baby's gurgling stopped.